MW01275423

INADEQUACIES

STORIES

J. MICHAEL MORRIS JR.

STEPHEN F. AUSTIN STATE UNIVERSITY PRESS

For more information:
Stephen F. Austin State University Press
P.O. Box 13007 SFA Station
Nacogdoches, Texas 75962
sfapress@sfasu.edu
www.sfasu.edu/sfapress

Managing Editor: Kimberly Verhines
Book design: Katt Noble
Cover Design: Katt Noble

Distributed by Texas A&M Consortium
www.tamupress.com

ISBN: 978-1-62288-931-0

For my daughter,
Vivienne.

James Morris

CONTENTS

THE LIFEGUARD

IT'S NOT ALWAYS EASY TO KNOW where to start with a story like this, especially since no one can agree on when it all really began. Most people would tell you that it started on that September day when Allison stepped onto the bridge. Others would point to a generation ago when Joshua's family moved into the area and his father became a frequent resident of the Sheriff department's drunk tank. But most of those people will be missing the point. It started with a sign.

Long after the sheriff's department had grown accustomed to regular calls to the Jordan house and after their mother was buried, and after the father finally ran off for good, everyone knew about Joshua Jordan's fondness for signs. The first sign was taken the night before Joanie Jordan shipped off to boot camp. As the fifteen-year-old Joshua stood guard, his sister Joanie scaled the fence around a warehouse that had been abandoned for so long that no one could remember what used to be there. A lot of signs would come later, but that first one was a rusty rectangle that declared "private property" in big block letters. After Joanie left him alone in that cramped one-bedroom apartment they'd barely been able to afford, Joshua hung the sign on the wall waiting for her to return. When she didn't return, more signs started disappearing around town.

It was the sheriff who caught Joshua that day in late September. Driving by the community pool that had been shut down and drained for the winter, she saw a skinny teenager move behind the fence. As he tried to pry an old sign from the wall, Joshua heard the sheriff hop the side of the chain-link fence. Joshua had gotten too confident, and there was nowhere for him to go. A lot of people think they know how the conversation went after Joshua was caught, picturing it as though they had been there planted against a wall. They like to picture some grizzled old hardass who'd try to put the fear of God into Joshua, but the sheriff at the time couldn't have been more different.

For one thing, she heard the stories about Joanie Jordan that reminded her about so many other soldiers she'd seen laid to rest. Joanie hadn't joined up for glory and she hadn't joined up because she believed all the recruitment ads on TV. Like so many others, she joined up because it was the only way people like them would ever be anything more than people like them. The sheriff drove back to the station, maybe picturing Joanie signing the papers with every intention that she'd send for Joshua once she could secure a post somewhere stateside. There were a handful of stories about why Joanie never came back, but the most popular one involves Joanie on a patrol not long after arriving overseas in some desert. Would she have felt anything when her Humvee hit the IED? Or would she have just felt the world shift under her, and then think of Joshua alone in that apartment? The sheriff had been at the funeral the day Joanie was laid to rest, paying her respects without saying anything to Joshua. She made an appearance anytime a soldier was buried, but the image of Joshua Jordan sitting alone at the graveyard to receive a folded flag stuck in her head. Instead of the interrogation room with the stiff metal chairs, Joshua was taken to the sheriff's office and given a soda while he waited.

When the sheriff finally walked in, she took a seat behind her desk. "Why are these signs so important to you, Joshua?" She let the question sit between them on her desk. Not every type of sign had gone missing. It was only the minor signs, the ones no one would miss, that seemed to vanish. While every stop sign and deer sign remained untouched, everyone understood that a sign for a private parking spot was fair game.

He didn't say anything. Maybe he was surprised to find someone who thought the disappearance of signs was about anything more than some kid trying to test the boundaries of authority. Joshua had always known what it was like to grow up with so much less than everyone else; before she left, Joanie reminded him that the rusted old sign set them apart. The other kids at school had new backpacks each year and winter coats that fit right, but only Joshua had a collection of signs hanging in his small one-bedroom apartment.

"I don't think you're a bad kid," the sheriff leaned forward.

"You're too young to be bad, but you won't be young forever. There are guys in the county jail that I used to coach in soccer and women who used to sell Girl Scout cookies outside church. No one is born bad, but we can all get there if we aren't careful."

"Am I being arrested?"

"No, Joshua. I don't think arresting you will do any good." The sheriff stood up, holding the door open for him. "As you walk home, you should start thinking about who you want to be."

There weren't many people walking around that September day when Joshua left the station. It wouldn't start snowing for another month or two, but the brisk air had already begun to dip into the forties in preparation for a crisp autumn. Even though it would have made more sense for Joshua to walk through the center of town to get back to his apartment, he began walking along the edges of town and kept going. Beyond the factory that had closed down a few years ago and past streets of boarded-up businesses, Joshua walked toward the thick trees in the distance and thought of Joanie. She had taught him how to swim, after their mother passed. Helping him navigate the river in the summer, she taught him how dangerous it could be in the fall. Joanie had always loved the water, and the young Joshua had grown into a fierce swimmer in his efforts to keep pace with her. So he might have walked into the woods, wanting to be surrounded by the sound of water rushing downstream.

Not many people know about this town, but everyone knows about that bridge. The only way across the river for miles, trying to find another bridge to cross would add at least fifty miles to any trip. The river snakes deep into the Oregon countryside in both directions, disappearing into the trees. The Oregon Department of Transportation shut that bridge down for a month once, to work on the structural integrity; losing the normally steady stream of travelers almost put the local gas station and supermarket out of business. That bridge was a familiar sight to anyone in town, standing in the background like just another mountain. What wasn't familiar was the sight of anyone standing out on the bridge, and that's what Joshua saw as he turned back toward town.

A figure in a dark coat stood on the white bridge, her body so clear against the grey sky. She stood there looking out over the water, not moving as Joshua watched from a distance. This might not have been so strange in and of itself, but Joshua continued watching the woman as she stepped onto the edge of the bridge's rounded railing. He couldn't have known at the time that the figure in the distance was Allison Adams, a singer desperately seeking what she considered a beautiful ending. Jumps from that bridge had always been rare. Allison didn't know what all the locals did: that a fall from one hundred and thirty feet is not the quick and certain end that drove her to step out onto that railing.

As Allison stood on the railing, Joshua didn't move from the overlook downstream from the bridge. Poised and delicate, did

Allison look in Joshua's direction as she stepped off the railing? Did she seem to hang in mid-air for a moment, as her eyes locked with his? Whichever way it went, her body dipped below the water's surface as quickly as if Joshua had imagined her to begin with.

Most people would have instinctively run toward the bridge, to scream for help as the water carried the woman into the distance. Joshua didn't do this though, having learned from an early age how quickly the water churned this time of year. He ran away from the bridge, heading down the sloping hillside along the water's edge.

Though Allison had fallen straight down from the bridge, she emerged from the water almost fifty yards downstream. The swift current carried her beyond any obstacles, as the water's oppressive cold hit her all at once. No matter what drives a person to step off a bridge, some people will say that the regret comes instantly—this overwhelming force to survive, in the face of everything that led up to that last step off the bridge. So Allison's arms and legs struggled against the water, feeling heavier each time she managed to push her head back above the water's surface. She tried to grab onto rocks and roots as the water shoved her forward, but failed each time to make her fingers close around anything at all. As her body slowed, Allison saw a glimpse of a figure in the distance on the shore. Had her body not been shocked by the cold, she would have recognized the sight of a teenage boy stripping off everything but his underwear before diving into the river.

When her head dipped below the water, the cold had already seeped into Allison so fully that she barely registered any panic. She might have thought that this was a fitting ending, to find herself regretting this last choice after hundreds of other regretted choices. And then she felt something connect with her body, and lift her head above the frothy water. Wrapping one of her cold and lifeless arms around his shoulder, the boy swam as best he could toward the shore. His arms were wiry and lean, and she only had a moment to wonder why he wasn't wearing any clothes. She could barely remember that she had arms at this point, but this boy (or teenager?) moved his arms with a single-minded purpose that seemed to defy the chill creeping so deeply into her. By the time he got them to the rocky shore of the river, the young man's body was cut and bruised as he dragged her to safety. As her body rose from the water, Allison could only think of how tired she was and how nice it might feel to close her eyes and sleep for a while.

Neither Joshua nor Allison would have known about the driver in the distance who also saw her drop from the bridge. By the time the driver connected with 911, Allison's body would have already been out of sight and carried out into the wilderness. When the ambulance and the sheriff's cars pulled out of town, maybe they thought it was already too late.

The sirens got closer as Joshua somehow managed to run back to where he left his clothes. Flinging his wet underwear into the woods, Joshua pulled on his dry pants and shirt to keep some of the September chill at bay. He pulled his socks and shoes back on, but left his coat in his hands as he ran back to the woman. By the time the Sheriff arrived downstream from the bridge, the sky had begun to darken; the flashing lights of the patrol cars cast an eerie glow over the water, as sounds began to emerge from further down the river.

The sheriff led a trio of deputies through the darkening forest, their flashlights cutting slivers of light into the woods until they saw Joshua struggling to carry the woman in his arms. His body must have been ready to finally give out on him, the adrenaline running empty and the chilled air slowing him down as he tried to take another step. They rushed toward him, to find the woman wrapped in his coat barely breathing. As one deputy ran back to get the EMTs and blankets, the others rushed forward to help the woman and Joshua. "I got her out of the water," he said, before his legs buckled and the deputies helped him toward the ambulance lights.

Later that night, while Allison slept in her hospital bed, Joshua and the sheriff sat together in the nurse's breakroom. The cafeteria was already closed for the night, but they sat at a small table over Styrofoam cups of coffee and a few bags of pretzels. Joshua had been checked out by the EMTs and driven to the hospital in the sheriff's car, but there was no sense in admitting him for a few scrapes.

"I knew I was right about you," the sheriff said, but Joshua stared down at his coffee. "Not many people would have jumped into the water to save a stranger."

"I don't know," Joshua said quietly, mostly to himself.

"I do," she said. "I've seen enough to know." The sheriff had already started to do her homework on him. She'd swung by the high school not long after he left the station. Her idea of him already started to form before she got the call about the bridge, picturing the quiet kid trying to make it to the end of the day as best he could, eating his peanut butter and jelly sandwiches alone outside of the cafeteria.

"So what happens now?"

"I spoke with the doctor. The woman will be alright after a little rest, but you've both had a night."

"What happens to me?" Joshua asked, fiddling with his bag of pretzels.

Of all the stories about Joanie's death, the only thing that really matters is that the news came on a Tuesday: the Tuesday before Joshua turned sixteen. Here's why that matters: In the state of Oregon, you need to be at least sixteen years old to petition to become an emancipated minor. If anyone had been around, they'd have seen the wheels in motion when Joshua received that death notice in the mail – maybe he knew that public school teachers are mandatory reporters in Oregon, or maybe he just worried about one call to Child Protective Services for some well-intentioned social worker to start determining what was best for him. After everything Joshua had seen with his own parents, who could blame him for assuming that foster parents wouldn't be any better? Since the day he arrived at the county courthouse with paperwork for emancipation, Joshua had been getting himself to school and buying his own groceries with what little remained of Joanie's final paycheck. Even though the law would have seen two adults drinking coffee in the harsh hospital light, he must have looked young and scared as he wondered if he had finally brought too much attention to himself.

"Well, that's what I wanted to talk to you about." The sheriff paused to take a drink of her coffee, and for a moment the rest of the hospital floor probably felt a bit too quiet. "You live in an apartment along Third Street, right?"

"Yeah." Joshua wouldn't have mentioned that he only had a few months' rent left and was worried about what would happen when that money ran out. Not everyone knows this part, but Joshua didn't end up getting anything in the way of the army death benefit. He should have gotten $100,000 for losing his sister on active duty, but it didn't work out like that. Maybe Joanie had listed their dad as next of kin, not wanting anyone to ask questions; maybe that money got lost in bureaucracy that Joshua didn't know to fight against. The sheriff might have known all about how close Joshua was to losing the last bit of comfort he had, but maybe their conversation would have gone the same way no matter what.

"You see, my sister-in-law was telling me a few days ago about this problem she can't seem to solve. You know those rental cabins being developed up along the river?" The sheriff continued once she saw Joshua nod. "Well, she's part of that whole job, and things are moving at a snail's pace. As soon as the snow hits, they'll have to shut down construction and only one of the cabins is finished; the rest will be lucky to have the exteriors done by the time the construction crew leaves for the winter. What she needs is someone reliable to live onsite and keep an eye on things. Nothing too crazy, just someone to run the heat in the cabins with indoor plumbing, and make sure animals don't move in over the winter. She's been having a hard time finding a caretaker she can trust, and until today I hadn't thought of anyone."

"You mean me?"

"Yeah." The sheriff probably smiled at him, something between the mother he barely remembered and the sister he couldn't stop thinking about. "Only if you stay in high school though, and graduate."

"For how long?"

"This winter at least, but maybe it'll turn into a long-term position after the cabins are all done. There's always something to be looked after, if you're the type." The sheriff extended her hand across the small table, Joshua tentatively shaking it as he finished the rest of his bitter coffee. It just took an interview with the sheriff's sister-in-law to finalize everything, mostly just to make sure that Joshua seemed above board. If there were any concerns about work permits for a 16-year-old living alone, surely his status as an emancipated minor would have kept that from being a problem. He moved into the caretaker's cabin just a few weeks later, filling a linen closet with a mix of his sister's things and a collection of signs.

Allison woke up that night after Joshua and the sheriff had both left the hospital, asking a nurse about the young man who saved her. Allison didn't get any information. So instead, she began to craft her own ideas of Joshua without even a name as a starting point. As her memories mixed with the medication, she saw the strong young arms battling against the river; she felt herself lift out of the water again, feeling arms steadier than any she could remember. For the first time in a long time, she almost felt as though someone would take care of her. As though someone wanted to be there for her. Not because she might appeal to the right demographics, but because that's just what some people do.

Joshua never spoke with Allison or even saw her again; he only even learned her name weeks after everything happened, once the story had begun to move through the town under its own power. He learned about the young woman smarter than anyone wanted to acknowledge;

the pretty young girl who had grown into a stunning young woman with a voice that made people look up from their coffees when she first took the stage at local open mics all those years ago.

Maybe the story would have ended here, except that Allison felt transformed by her experience. And through this transformation, the first album she released of her own music later that year had an energy that no one expected. She walked away from anyone who hadn't supported her and built an army of fans all on her own. Over the course of the next eighteen months as Joshua quietly watched over the development of cabins and kept to himself, Allison took every opportunity to talk about what happened. She talked about how she had filled notebooks with song after song of heartfelt and moving lyrics, later realizing that her label only wanted her to sing pop songs proven to appeal to her designated demographic of pre-teen girls. Allison spoke about how stepping onto that bridge seemed at the time like the only way for her to seize control again, remembering a river between Portland and Redding from those long drives her family had taken when she was little. She had been fortunate enough to experience rebirth at the hands of her own personal lifeguard, saving her in all the ways that we can be saved. She wanted others to be inspired by her own transformation, which never would have happened had she not taken that step off the bridge. Though she never reached stardom, her music circulated freely across the country through small communities of ardent fans.

It was nearly two years before anyone stepped out onto that bridge again, nearly two years before the young caretaker of the cabins on the outskirts of town felt drawn back into that river. Though Joshua's cabin had a small box of liberated signs in a linen closet, the town had long ago stopped needing to replace signs. He was still that same kid who ate his peanut butter and jelly sandwiches alone, except for a standing coffee appointment with the sheriff twice a week. His grades had improved, and the world seemed willing to leave him to his solitude in the cabins, until Allison died in a tragic car crash. The twenty-three-year-old's death drove her most zealous fans to seek the same rebirth she had found, and they all knew about the lifeguard.

When it happened again, Joshua didn't even know about Allison's recent death. He had been on the porch of the caretaker's cabin, spending a Saturday trying to find the energy to care about those last assignments of his senior year, before the high school's graduation ceremony. It was a warm June day, and he had been about to make a sandwich for lunch when he looked in the direction of the bridge to see a car pull off the road. A young couple stepped out onto the bridge, and Joshua stood up from his chair to watch them. As they walked out into the middle of the bridge, Joshua began cautiously making his way down to the water. By the time he was near the water's edge, he saw the two figures standing on the railing. They looked around, perhaps for him. Joshua reached for his cell phone to call the sheriff but stopped as he saw the couple step out into the air and plummet toward the water.

This time, the water wasn't shockingly cold, and the current was less ferocious. Joshua was able to pull the woman out of the water first, before going back in for her boyfriend. The three of them laid on the shore, until Joshua caught his breath enough to call the sheriff and tell her what happened. The next day, a sign was placed on the bridge warning of a fine and possible jail time for violating the state statute of jumping off public bridges. None of the people who followed in Allison's footsteps knew about Joshua in any real sense, but it wouldn't have made a difference even if they did. Allison's stories of rebirth and renewal promised a new beginning for any willing to take the leap; a single mistake that turned out to be the best choice she could have made. This promise of clarity had a way of dispelling all the danger, as though the mysterious lifeguard was all it took to keep death at bay. Allison's untimely death finalized the transformation that started the moment Joshua pulled her from the water; after all, no self-respecting messiah ever gets to die of old age.

Over the course of the summer, more people came. After that first couple, there were four other separate incidents of couples jumping from the bridge. They always came in pairs, clinging onto one another as they fell. Each person he dragged from the water found a new energy for their lives, seeing any injuries sustained as a small price to pay for being transformed like Allison had been. Joshua did not have a say in these jumps, and no publicized warnings or threats from the sheriff made any difference for those seeking their own transformation. When deputies would drive by the bridge on the lookout for any potential jumpers, it would be easy for someone to keep driving and circle back after the patrol car left. The sheriff tried to get a camera installed on the bridge, but the proposal was rejected as another expense the town couldn't afford. Ultimately, the threat seemed to be to the jumpers themselves. No one was encouraging this kind of recklessness, but the town couldn't be held responsible for the ideas that percolate in the minds of the sad and lonely. As was usually the case, the sheriff seemed to be the only one who thought about Joshua through all this.

The final jump was just after the second anniversary of Allison's rebirth, with the air turning sharp and crisp. Joshua had taken a rare trip away from the cabins, to go into town for shopping and a coffee with the sheriff. She was up for re-election but didn't want to talk about it. On the drive back to the cabins, Joshua saw a lone figure on the bridge. In the fading light, he might have sworn that it was Joanie perched on the railing. He called the sheriff as he pulled the car over, running onto the bridge and leaving the phone on the front seat behind him. The distance between them would have felt vast, the patch of bridge lit up by his car's headlights. Stepping from the dirt road onto the old metal bridge, Joshua saw that the woman's hair was darker than Joanie's, but she looked to be the age his sister had been that last time he saw her. Maybe he thought of an old memory from when there were still two Jordan kids, and how the "private property" sign hung in his caretaker's cabin. Maybe he only thought of the metal bridge under his feet, each step feeling tentative as he approached the woman.

"Are you him?" The woman shouted out over the wind, as she eyed the river warily.

"Who?" Joshua walked toward her.

"The lifeguard," she said.

"No." Joshua looked at her, watching how shaky her legs looked on top of the railing. "I'm just a guy."

"I think you're lying," she smiled, "You look the way everyone describes."

"It doesn't matter who I am," Joshua said, almost within arm's reach of her now.

"You're the one who saves people," she said, as confident in this as she was in the darkening sky overhead. "That's good. I'm going to need you to save me, ok?"

"Look, I don't know what you've heard. People can die jumping off this bridge." Joshua must have turned around when he heard the sirens, seeing the familiar cherries-and-berries in the distance.

"But they don't," The woman looked down at the water, "because you're here to save them."

"They're wrong about me." Joshua reached out toward her, trying to will her to grab a hold of his hand and step off the railing.

"I don't think so. I can see who you really are," she said, leaning off of the bridge and falling forward as the sheriff's car drew closer.

A lot of people will tell you that the woman stepped off the bridge and Joshua hesitated for just a moment. They'll say he had begun to feel the weight of responsibility bearing down on him, that expectation of being the pivotal moment in someone else's life. They'll paint it as the final moment that has a way of sealing one's fate. But that's not how it went. There was no hesitation.

As he jumped from that height, Joshua felt the regret that so many others had talked about. This leap was different from the times he'd dove in at the shore, feeling the chill night air as the water rushed toward him. It was a single-minded certainty that he had made a mistake, causing him to second guess everything about himself right before the water swallowed him whole. His drop from the bridge sent Joshua almost to the river floor. His lungs burned as he scrambled to swim back to the top, and he might not have thought he would make it until he finally burst through the surface of the water gasping in the evening light. As his legs kicked against the water and his arms paddled to keep him afloat, he scanned the water for the young woman. She was just ahead of him, her head falling below the surface before kicking herself up just enough. She had only a moment to scream, before disappearing again under the water. This wasn't how it was supposed to be.

In all of the rescues, Joshua's arms never had to work so hard against the shock of the cold and the pounding water. He had never been this tired, this out of breath, as he swam toward the woman. She resurfaced again, for just a moment, just enough time for Joshua to crash into her as she submerged. She was barely conscious by the time Joshua pulled her up. The water shuffled and pushed them around, as Joshua kicked to keep them both above the surface now. When the river bent, he took the chance to angle toward the patch of submerged trees he knew lay at that part of the river; he braced himself just before the water turned into the trees, catching a trunk with his whole body.

The force of the impact dislodged the woman from him, and her eyes were more alert now. She closed her hand around his one free hand, the rest of Joshua's body clinging to the tree trunk. Had anyone gotten close enough, they would have seen Joshua's left arm straining to pull the woman toward him; muscles willing to tear themselves in two if it somehow meant that he could be stronger than the current. A bystander would have seen the terror in his eyes, as Joshua realized that he would never be strong enough. It wasn't terror in her eyes though, it was something else. Maybe it was acceptance as her fingers slipped from his grip, or maybe the faith that led her to step out onto the railing had fully dissipated and left nothing behind. The sheriff made it down to the river just in time to watch the woman float away from Joshua, and the body wouldn't be found for another 15 months. It would end up so far downriver that a string of park rangers and sheriffs would have to turn to their phone tree to find out where the young woman had come from.

This time, the sheriff didn't take Joshua to the hospital. He wasn't badly hurt, and it might not have seemed worth it to just go through the motions yet another time. After she helped pull him from the water, he dried off with a blanket she kept in the car, smelling like the spare tire and car jack it had been wrapped around for months. She took him to get his car and followed him back to the caretaker's cabin. She sat in the kitchen while he changed into dry clothes, ignoring the rusted "private property" sign that Joshua threw a dish towel over when she came to visit. Coming back out to brew coffee in silence, Joshua knew how she liked her coffee by this point (two creams, one sugar) and placed it in front of her. As he sat down with his own cup (two creams, no sugar), they each waited for the other one to speak.

They both ended up waiting a while.

"It wasn't your fault," she said finally, after a long drink from her mug. It was shaped like a cow, some secondhand house-warming gift she gave him after he first moved into the place. "It's not fair what they've done to you, Joshua. Turning you into some mythic figure who's here just to ease the burdens from their shoulders. It's not your responsibility to fix them."

"If I don't, then who will?" He asked quietly.

"Maybe no one, sometimes." She shrugged. "I wish it weren't that way, but not everyone gets the help they need. And the cruelest part of being good at helping people is feeling like you can save everyone, and then having to learn that it just doesn't work out like that. It never will, no matter how much of yourself you give."

Joshua took a drink from his cup, remaining silent for a moment.

"Have you ever thought about who you are, Sheriff? I don't think I ever have. I've always had to focus more on who I'm not, and whether I'm different from what people say about me."

"You're old enough now that none of that needs to matter. These cabins, this town, that river, they can all survive without you if that's what you want."

After finishing her coffee, the sheriff stood up and placed a gentle hand on his shoulder. For a second, they both let it sit there before she left his cabin and closed the door behind her. In two weeks, she'd be voted out as sheriff; maybe she already had a sense that things would play out this way, but that night she was more focused on heading back to the station and writing up another report about that damn bridge.

There are a dozen stories about what happened next and why, but no one argues with the facts. The next day on the other side of the Idaho border, someone reported that a sign went missing from a community pool. Whether it was the same sign or not, a similar sign appeared on the bridge a few days later; it was fastened tight with metal bands and placed high enough that it would have taken a little too much effort to remove. The sheriff's sister-in-law began looking for a new caretaker that next week, and anyone who set foot out on that bridge after the last week of September would be able to look up and see a sign that read "No Lifeguard on Duty."

INCANTATIONS

MARY DIDN'T WANT TO THINK about how many people saw her standing in the parking lot, locking a car that was already locked. She tried to not focus on that right now, tried not to think about how her ringing phone shook the random collection of items in her purse. It was the second time she had pressed the button on her keys, the quick beep-beep of the car horn trying to reassure her that the car was locked. This had not helped.

There were no memories of how far back it went, but she sometimes imagined herself as a small girl, meticulously checking the lights in her room and throughout the house before she felt ready to leave for preschool. Maybe nightlights had been unplugged to prevent a fire or the faucet had been triple-checked to avoid flooding the house – whatever it took to relieve that weight in her chest when things felt just a bit off. It sometimes helped to think that she always needed a level of certainty that most people found excessive, rather than speculating about some initial moment that set years of worry in motion.

On the fourth time, it felt different. She could feel the weight in her chest fade with the beep of the car and flash of the taillights. There was a comfort in knowing that her car was as locked as it could be, helping chase away visions of an unlocked car being easy prey for the burglars who only existed in her mind. Mary let out a deep breath and turned toward the hospital. In her purse, the phone rang one last time before falling silent.

By the time she got to her dad's pre-op room, he was already wearing the baggy sweatpants for surgery. A duffel bag sat on the lone chair in the room, and he moved it to the floor as he saw her approach. The TV was on, but he turned his focus toward her.

"It'll probably be a bit longer." He grinned big, as though trying to sell her a car. Low mileage of course, with an engine as reliable as a workhorse.

"Sorry I'm late." Mary looked down at her feet.

"Don't worry about it, Kiddo." Another big grin. He did this sort of thing a lot, not asking why she was late. They both knew why.

She looked down at her watch. It was 10:16, and his surgery had been planned for ten o'clock. "Did they tell you how long the wait will be?"

"No idea, but you know how busy these doctors are." He turned his focus back toward the TV, flipping through channels.

"Hopefully not much longer then." Mary set her purse on her lap, trying to ignore the missed call.

"It's alright," her dad said, "I've got plenty of time." He continued changing the channels, only stopping to admire the occasional car commercial.

"So everything's ready for your surgery?" She chose to not ask about the lightheadedness or if there were any new developments since his original diagnosis. If she wrote down every question that went unasked between them, how long before those questions would fill a book? How long before they would fill a shelf?

"Couldn't be better. I'll be good as new in no time." That smile again, honed from years of convincing people that he was on their side. It was never only about making the sale; he wanted to get you into the right car. That smile told people that he was looking out for them, that he knew it would all work out.

"Ok." Mary reached inside her purse for the phone and saw that the missed call was from Samuel. Mary's focus turned to the large sign in the room forbidding cell phone use. She turned off her phone and placed it back in her purse.

"This is all pretty routine," her dad said, watching a family on TV marvel at the safety features of their new SUV. "Probably even boring compared to what these surgeons normally do."

"Is that why I'm the only one here? Did you even tell anyone else?"

"I told Linda about the surgery." Linda was Mary's third stepmother, and the only one her dad still talked to despite the trial separation. "But I'm not going to bother your mom yet. Besides, I figured that you were worrying enough for both of you."

Mary sighed. "Why isn't Linda here then, if she knows?"

"Well, I didn't tell her everything. She thinks the surgery is in two weeks, but that's just so she won't panic." Another change of the channel. "You're the responsible one in the family anyways, so why would anyone else need to be here?"

"You should tell Linda before you go under."

"I'll surprise her with the good news after I wake up." His confidence was unflappable, sturdy in the face of everything he couldn't predict. The monthly payment might be more than you want, but this car is an investment in the future. "It'll be good news."

BEFORE SHE KNEW WHY, MARY sensed that something was wrong when she felt that pressure in her chest and an inability to move away from needing to be certain. Her brain worked differently, and both of her parents had their way of processing the problem. From an early age, Mary could identify the frustration in her mom's eyes any time Mary's brain just couldn't move on. Where her mom saw a problem, Mary's dad instead saw a quirk so minor as not to be worth mentioning. He must have come up with the term *incantations*, but any actual memory had long ago been warped into the type of family legend Mary suspected was mostly false. In dwelling on the problem or ignoring the problem, Mary's parents each had their way of just compounding it all. Neither offered help, only their own way of dealing with a daughter who fell short.

Mary didn't want to be a problem to be solved or dealt with and learning to hide that part of herself became as natural as anything else. Her mom stopped talking about taking Mary to a special doctor, and her dad willfully ignored those small moments where Mary failed to hide it. Maybe Mary's mom just wanted to believe that these sorts of problems could go away on their own; even though he'd never admit it, Mary suspected that her dad felt the same way too. Either way, Mary had grown used to feeling that weight in her chest and finding a way to relieve it all on her own.

When she was sixteen, moments of stress made it too much to ignore. During Junior Year finals, she found herself unable to leave for school without the dread of an unlocked door tempting robbers or a gas oven leading to tragedy. Doors had been checked and double-checked, but that feeling in her chest wouldn't go away. She had felt paralyzed by the ticking of the clock, knowing she wouldn't be able to explain why the dread of something left undone wouldn't go away.

When Mary was seventeen, their family dog had gotten out when a gate had failed to fully close. The dog had come back after a few hours of roaming the neighborhood, but that hadn't been enough to keep Mary from thinking about how it just takes one careless driver for a loose dog to not come home. For weeks afterward, Mary checked every gate and door. Twice. Three times. Four times. Sometimes it went on for too long, until she found her friends calling to see why she was so late. Her boyfriend saw her as paranoid, giving her a hard time about it any time he saw her double-check a locked door or verify that the oven was off. She tried to explain it more than once, but the words always fell flat. She couldn't explain the weight in her chest or why it only came sometimes. She couldn't explain why it seemed to vanish for months at a time, until she became paralyzed with a fear that she hadn't properly turned off the stove. She didn't know where to start, so it was easier to not try.

Mary could go months without thinking about it too much, focusing instead on the normal routine of her life. Without that weight in her chest encroaching upon plans or priorities, she wanted to believe it wasn't serious. There were plenty of times it wasn't, until those times it was.

Her dad looked out into the hallway at the sound of foot traffic, as a nurse walked toward the room.

"Mr. Wilson?" The nurse stopped at the doorway; she was pretty and probably in her mid-twenties like Mary. "The surgical team is heading up here now."

"You know where to find me," Mary's dad said with a laugh. "See? Shouldn't be too long, Kiddo."

Mary always wondered if her dad's smile faded when he was alone. Did that car salesman confidence vanish behind closed doors, or was he always so sure of things working out in his favor?

There was a light knocking against the open door of the hospital room, and Mary turned to see a trio of doctors in surgical gear. She recognized Dr. Thorne, her dad's cardiothoracic surgeon. He had a kind face, with bits of grey coloring an otherwise deep maple head of hair.

Behind Dr. Thorne, the other two doctors were new. The doctors looked confident in their scrubs, and Mary could see a new nurse just outside the room waiting. Dr. Thorne stepped forward, offering his hand to both Mary and her dad.

"Good morning." Dr. Thorne stood taller than both of his colleagues. "I wanted to introduce you to some key members of our surgical team before everything starts."

Mary's dad shook Dr. Thorne's hand, as though they had become fast friends at the bar. Mary shook the outstretched hand quickly, only half-rising from her seat.

"Dr. Gomez will be your anesthesiologist and Dr. Wallace will be my surgical assistant." Dr. Thorne gestured toward his colleagues, who both nodded silently. "We'll also be assisted by several nurses, but it can be hard to gather a full surgical team at once. We wanted to take a moment to answer any final questions you might have about the surgery."

"I'm ready, Doc." Mary's dad smiled at all three doctors.

"That's great. We're just waiting for an O.R. to open up, and I expect we can plan on the surgery itself starting up at 11."

After the doctors left, the nurse led Mary out into the waiting room so her dad could prepare for surgery. Mary held her purse tight, as she walked through the winding hallways.

Senior year of college, Mary met Samuel for the first time. Mary's roommate sequestered herself and Samuel away in her room, so they could focus on a group project for a class. There never seemed to be anything more between them than a Sociology project, but Mary always wondered if her roommate wanted there to be.

Mary's roommate had chosen to not talk about the bedtime routine that had arisen when Mary felt the weight of her classes bearing down on her that semester. Mary began to check each knob on the stove, counting to herself and tapping the handle of the oven. One-two-three-four. Tap-Tap. One-two-three-four. Tap-Tap. Her roommate ignored it.

It had been one night toward the end of her senior year, and Mary would have smelled like sweat after a long day of school and work. She remembered thinking that Samuel was still in her roommate's room, not noticing when he left to use the shared bathroom. Mary's routine had gone on for two minutes. Four minutes.

She couldn't turn away from the oven, that weight in her chest making her certain that something was left undone.

One-two-three-four. Tap-Tap.

She didn't know why, but something wasn't letting this go. A 10-second process stretching into five minutes and then six.

Was it that paper she still needed to work on?

One-two-three-four. Tap-Tap.

Was it her boyfriend, who only recently turned into more of an asshole without any apparent reason?

One-two-three-four. Tap-Tap.

"Fuck." She remembered muttering, feeling the time pass by. She was tired. She just wanted to get rid of that weight in her chest, so she could sleep.

One-two-three-four. Tap-Tap.

When she heard the toilet flush, Mary turned around to see Samuel leaving the bathroom.

"Is everything good, Mary?"

"Yeah, it's just--. I've got to check things before bed."

He had smiled then, a smile so different from the ones she had become accustomed to anytime someone new saw this side of her. It wasn't a *you're-a-freak* smile or a *this-is-in-your-head* smile or a *just-an-incantation* smile. He walked over and ran his hand a few inches above each of the burners, eyeing all the knobs in their off positions.

"Everything looks good to me." That had been all it took. After Samuel had gone back to the group project, Mary let out a deep breath. It was sometimes hard to say why the weight in her chest faded.

SITTING DOWN IN THE WAITING ROOM, Mary removed a pile of papers from her purse. She placed her purse on the small table next to her, unfolding the printed pages that contained everything she needed to know about aortic valve disease. Mary looked around the room at the other people waiting, each of them trying to find some level of comfort in the stiff hospital chairs. With nurses, doctors, and orderlies moving through the small room, Mary shifted her attention down to the stack of papers in her hands.

It all started almost three months ago, after her dad fainted when they met up for coffee. He tried to shrug it off, but Mary pushed him to make an appointment with his doctor. She was there with her dad two months ago, for that initial appointment. Mary knew the odds were good he would have found a reason to put it off if she hadn't taken time to be at the appointment with him, and he could have found reasons to keep putting it off. She had been with her dad for that first appointment with Dr. Thorne, and later when the tests came back to reveal that one of the valves of her dad's heart had aortic stenosis: a tightening of the valve that hinders blood flow, sometimes leading to fainting. Dr. Thorne had moved quickly, sliding Mary's dad into a cancellation slot to avoid additional risks the longer they waited.

During that first hour in the waiting room, Mary read everything about the surgery. Her dad would be under full anesthesia at this point, and as many as fifteen people might be in the room for his surgery. Each person would monitor some part of the process, or watch one of a handful of machines. This type of surgery could take as long as six hours, and even experienced surgeons would say it depended on what they found once they got in there.

During the second hour, Mary folded the stack of printed pages back into her purse. She picked up a National Geographic magazine, trying to distract herself with stories about changing migration patterns or how domestication led to physical changes in early wolves.

When she could no longer ignore the fact that she hadn't eaten all day, Mary grabbed her things and went to the hospital café. Sitting on a bench outside the hospital with her muffin and coffee, she pulled her phone from her purse and turned it back on. She had a new voicemail, and she knew it would be from Samuel before she started listening to it.

"Hey Mary, I'm sure everything will go well today. I'll be around if you need anything." She erased the message after it was done, looking down at her phone as she chewed on her muffin. Maybe she should text him back? She started a message, thumb hovering over the letters. She pressed down on the "h," before erasing it. Finishing her muffin, Mary brought up Samuel's contact information in the phone.

She could call Samuel, and he'd find something to say that might make her feel better. He'd at least try, if she let him. Everyone else seemed to expect her to take care of everything: to organize the appointments, to make the lists, to be the rock. For as long as she could remember, Mary had been the responsible one. Her shoulders could be leaned on.

It was nice to not be the rock sometimes.

She almost pressed the call button before changing her mind, turning off the phone.

After Mary finished her business degree, she found a new place close to the entry-level bank job she'd landed. It would be almost a year before she saw Samuel again, working at a bar near her office. Her whole week had been building up to the first big presentation of her career, and it didn't help that her boss seemed incapable of clear direction. The weight of it grew in her chest.

When a few coworkers invited her out for a drink, Mary hoped that it might help her stop thinking about the presentation. She saw Samuel right away, pouring drinks with the white sleeves of his button-up shirt rolled to the elbow. He had grown out a short beard and moved quickly behind the bar as he mixed drinks. There was a flash of recognition as soon as Samuel saw her.

Mary remembered the way Samuel had casually looked around for his manager before making her a free drink. As he poured from the sifter to the stemmed glass, his fingers had twitched slightly as though casting a spell. She told him about everything that had happened since graduation and how she liked living on her own; he told her about how he stumbled into being a bartender during college, and found he liked it better than any of his prospects after graduation. Over the next few hours, she had a chance to not think about the impending presentation and whether or not her font choices were right. Even as her coworkers trickled away, Mary stayed a little longer to talk with Samuel about all the finer points of making a good cocktail.

Mary found more reasons to go to the bar, even after her coworkers found some new place they liked better. On those nights she didn't feel like drinking, Samuel would teach her about the craft that went into artisan cocktails. With his sleeves rolled up to show an expanding collection of tattoos, he taught her the right way to mix a margarita and introduced her to a growing list of drinks she never would have thought to try.

Over the next year, Mary developed a pattern that always found a way to repeat itself. A new boyfriend would be handsome and nice and say all the right things about liking Mary for who she was, not fully understanding what that entailed. Patience has a way of running out, and Mary saw that time and time again when a new boyfriend came to realize that she brought complications. Some of them tried to ignore that side of her, and others seemed to think they could fix her. All those relationships ended in one way or another, leading Mary back to that bar with Samuel to learn about the difference between bourbon and whiskey. When she started wiping down the tops of her glasses, he'd have a clean napkin ready. When the sound of the special martini spoon clinking around her glass seemed to calm her down, he'd casually slide it across the bar toward her.

Each time Samuel taught her about a new drink, Mary thought about how different he was from the men she dated. They never seemed to see beyond their own ideas of her, to see the woman underneath all the responsibility and professionalism. Samuel relaxed around her in a way most people never did, talking about things that mattered and didn't. Her boyfriends never randomly brought up philosophers while making a Moscow Mule, and never joked that a Philosophy degree made someone a better bartender. Several relationships ended, but Samuel stayed at the bar making drinks and referencing philosophers that Mary would try to look up on her phone without him noticing.

The night that her dad fainted, Mary told Samuel all about it. He listened until she felt like she had talked enough, and then he told her about his plans to make a drink in her honor:

One part orange juice.

Two shots of tequila.

Three parts pear juice.

Four maraschino cherries.

Finished off with two ceremonial taps on the bar.

Mary didn't know why she had laughed at that or why he could joke about things no one else could. She just knew that she felt seen without feeling scrutinized, and she knew that the weight in her chest pressed down on her a little less often when he was around.

BACK IN THE WAITING ROOM, it was getting close to hour five. Each time the door opened, she looked up hoping to see Dr. Thorne. A pile of read magazines was now stacked on her left and Mary found herself circling back to the printed pages about the surgery. At this rate, she felt almost prepared to assist with the surgery if it went on much longer.

At four o'clock, Mary thought about stepping away to call her mom. They barely talked anymore, and Mary had nothing to say, but at least someone else would be there.

At 4:10, she thought about calling Linda.

At 4:25, she thought about calling Samuel.

At 4:35, Mary looked up to see Dr. Thorne enter the waiting room. He undid his surgical mask slowly, looking tired.

She could feel a weight in her chest, as she waited for him to speak.

"It could not have gone better, Mary."

She exhaled.

"We're in the process of moving him into the ICU now, but everything is right on track. He'll have the breathing tubes removed over the next couple of hours, but you can sit with him once the ICU nurses have completed their initial intake evaluation."

"So, there weren't complications?"

"None," Dr. Thorne said, smiling. "If you're hungry, go and get some food. Maybe even leave the hospital for a bit; he'll likely be asleep for a while. Provided that everything continues at this same rate, you'll be able to sit with him in an hour or so."

Five weeks ago, she tried to leave her apartment to go to the store. She had stayed late at work but had forgotten to get groceries on her way home. She also needed to get her dad a card for Linda's birthday, because he would forget. He had always been able to forget about things, because her incantations never stood in the way of everything that needed to be done. Her incantations never stopped her from doing anything, they just made it harder.

On her way out of the apartment that night, something didn't feel right. The door was locked. She knew it was locked, but that weight in her chest was still there.

One-two-three-four. Tap-Tap.

Pulling on the door, to hear the bolt of the lock catch. Pressing against the door and tapping everything to keep it from swinging open while she was away.

One-two-three-four. Tap-Tap.

What time did the store close?

One-two-three-four. Tap-Tap.

It should be working, but it wasn't.

One-two-three-four. Tap-Tap.

It never took this long to make sure the door was closed.

One-two-three-four. Tap-Tap.

She eventually called Samuel, and he arrived to find her slumped against the door.

"Everything good?" He'd asked.

"No."

"That's ok too, sometimes." He shrugged, offering a hand to help her up.

On her feet, she checked the door one last time. One-two-three-four. Tap-Tap.

He offered to run errands with her, checking her car after they got out. Returning to her apartment later, she invited him in for a drink. Then two.

They sat on the couch, and she didn't have to worry about whether the door was locked or the stove was off or her car was secure.

As he stood up to leave, she kissed him. His arms closed around her securely as he pulled her in close for just a moment, before opening up again.

"I'm a mess," Mary said, not pulling away.

"I don't trust anyone who doesn't think they're a mess. That's how you know who isn't full of shit." Samuel gave her a kiss on the cheek, closing the door securely as he left. Mary heard him check the door to make sure it was locked, before his footsteps faded down the hallway. She walked toward the door to check it that night after he left, but the weight in her chest had already vanished. She fell asleep quickly that night.

Four weeks ago, Mary invited Samuel over. She told him all about her dad's aortic valve disease, and what the surgery looked like. Samuel made her a drink, and sat across from her on the couch. She told him how it had taken her twenty minutes to lock the apartment that morning.

One-two-three-four. Tap-Tap.

He listened as she explained it all, and she remembered thinking about everything Samuel hadn't done while she talked.

He hadn't tried to fix anything.

He hadn't told her it wasn't that bad.

He hadn't accused her of overreacting.

He just listened and offered to make her a new drink when hers was empty. Placing her drink on the coffee table, she moved over to Samuel. She straddled him on the couch, removing his shirt. She kissed him, pressing her body into his. In her bed later, Mary enjoyed the feeling of his arms around her.

While he slept, Mary's mind wandered. She imagined her mom's look of disappointment before Mary started hiding that part of herself, or how her dad shrugged away the incantations. She thought about the boyfriends who never stuck around long. Everyone had a way of dealing with Mary. How long would it be until Samuel started dealing with her too?

Three weeks ago, Mary cancelled plans with Samuel. She hadn't rescheduled, putting things off vaguely into the future. As Mary looked up everything her father would need to know and need to do for the surgery, she found reasons to avoid seeing Samuel. He'd text her something reassuring, not pushing in the way ex-boyfriends would have.

One-two-three-four. Tap-Tap.

One week ago, she had almost gone into the bar Samuel worked at. He would know all the right things to say or not say, content to teach her everything she'd need to know to make the perfect Manhattan if she didn't want to drink. She stood outside the bar for a minute, before changing her mind.

One-two-three-four. Tap-Tap.

Last night Samuel called, but Mary watched her phone buzz on the coffee table until it fell silent.

One-two-three-four. Tap-Tap.

Mary had been in bed that night, thinking about calling Samuel back. She thought about all of the people she had hoped would be different. The boyfriends who said they liked her or the friends who told her how great she was. She could count on one hand how many of those relationships still existed outside of occasional updates on social media. Samuel had been on that hand for so long, she didn't want to think about him not being there. She didn't want to think about all the ways she would fail to live up to his ideas of what a girlfriend should be.

One-two-three-four. Tap-Tap.

MARY COUNTED AT LEAST 3 SIGNS prohibiting cell phone use as a nurse guided her back into the ICU to sit with her dad. Thin blue sheets sectioned Mary and her dad off from everyone else in the ICU, but she could hear the constant shuffling of people moving around. Her dad wouldn't be able to move to his actual hospital room until his breathing tubes could be removed. Mary watched her dad as she sat down next to the bed, machines humming around him.

On the floor next to her dad's bed, Mary saw the black duffle bag. She bent down to unzip the bag. Resting on top of the folded clothes was a list in Mary's handwriting. New sweatpants and loose shirts with the tags still on, recommended clothing following heart surgery. Each item on the list had a sloppy line drawn through it. She zipped the bag, sliding it under her chair with the heel of her foot.

Even with the wires and low-grade caution of the ICU, Mary's dad slept with the same sense of assurance that clung to him through all his waking hours. If she could borrow some of that assurance he'd found so naturally, maybe she could ask others for help. She could call her mom or Linda, so she wouldn't have to be the only one there.

Or she could call Samuel, so she wouldn't have to be the rock.

Mary reached into her purse, dangling by its straps from the back of the stiff hospital chair. She removed her phone, looking at the dark and empty screen. As she held her phone, Mary thought of all the ways Samuel had helped her and the ways he seemed ready to keep helping her.

Everyone seemed ready at first, until they saw what that meant.

Until they were made to wait for Mary alone at parties and movies and weddings, because her brain refused to let the smallest worry evaporate so she could get on with her day. Until they couldn't do anything to make it better, because she couldn't do anything to make it better. Until even those who understood didn't really understand, because we all have limits. What would Samuel's limits be, and how long would it take for those limits to be tested?

And then Mary was outside of the hospital again, standing in front of the large automatic doors that led into the main reception area. She didn't have any new voicemails, but there was a new text from Samuel.

Let me know if you need anything. The message was simple, an offer to help if she'd let him. An offer to do something or nothing or just be there, if she'd let him.

I'm ok. Thanks. Mary texted back, before turning the phone off again. Letting out a deep breath as she placed the phone into her purse, Mary walked back inside the hospital.

One-two-three-four. Tap-Tap.

THE PERSISTANCE OF DOUBT

As I wake up, I don't recognize the SUV or remember how I got here. Stepping out of the green SUV, I can't even tell what time of day it is. The trees tower above me, and it could be late afternoon or early evening. There aren't any other cars parked here, and the lone SUV is parked at a small rest stop that looks to be carved out of the forest.

"Grace?" I look around, not even sure what I'm looking for. The SUV doesn't look familiar, but maybe it was a rental? I don't see my white truck, or Grace's red car anywhere. "Grace? Maura?"

Walking away from the SUV, I approach the front door of the small building. In the distance, there are only trees in any direction. As I walk closer to the small building, I look inside and there's no sign of Grace or Maura.

"Grace? Maura?" I say, as I walk inside. The large vending machines buzz against the wall, but I don't hear anything else. Grace must be in the bathroom and can't hear me. It would make sense if Maura was with her too; she wouldn't leave a four-year-old with me if I was sleeping. Why can't I remember though? Did something happen?

I exit the building and scan the small lot. It would be easy to lose track of where I am if not for the small building. All the trees look the same, and I haven't heard any cars drive by yet; I only hear the forest. As I stand by the side of the road looking into the distance, it occurs to me that I'm not sure how much time has passed. I can't help but wonder why there aren't a lot of people around. Maybe it's the off-season? I'm about to walk around the rest area again, but I see a young woman and her daughter emerge from a small block of trees just on the far side of the paved parking lot. For just a moment I hope that it's Grace and Maura, but the woman doesn't have Grace's red hair. I still get excited when I see them though, and I start walking in their direction. They'll at least be able to help me figure out where I am.

As I get closer, the woman and her little girl look familiar in a way that's hard to place. The woman has short brown hair and might be in her thirties like me. Her daughter looks to be about six or so, and she could be the spitting image of Grace; the little girl has the same brilliant red hair Grace does, walking with a kind of spring in her step that reminds me of Maura. As they get closer, the woman notices me and waves. I wave back, and for a moment I start to doubt whether they are strangers. The woman is talking with her daughter, but she smiles at me as they walk in my direction.

"Decided to check out the trail with us, after all? Sorry that it took us so long, but there's a nice little creek back there," the woman smiles at me in a way that feels so familiar.

"I…" They both look at me, and I just stop. Do they know me?

"Are we going to get to the camp soon, Grandpa?" The little girl rushes to hug my leg. "Can we still play some games today?"

I look down at the little girl, but I don't say anything at first. It's then that I look at my hands, noticing for the first time how tight the skin is around the bones. As I look up at the woman, I can see a look of concern start to form across her face.

"Are you feeling alright, Dad?" Maura asks. I look around the rest stop, and it comes back to me.

I look back down at Gracie, placing my hand on her shoulder. "I'd really like to play some games, Sweetie." I look back up at Maura, in time to see her shake the worry away. "I was starting to get a little stir crazy in the car, so I wanted to come to find you."

"Well, we're glad that you did. But I think we're ready to get back in the car, aren't we Grace?"

"What's stir crazy mean?" Gracie asks as we walk, reaching up to hold my hand.

"I just got a little bored after I woke up."

"Oh," She says with a firm understanding, "I get bored too."

I DON'T KNOW IF IT WAS THE FIRST TIME, but I like to tell myself it was. Maura had come over to borrow some of my tools, talking to me from the other room while I went into the kitchen. I had wanted to get us both some water, as things faded away. I don't know how much time passed, but I found myself a couple blocks away at a crosswalk. By the time Maura caught up with me, she was out of breath and looked panicked. What happened? Why did I just leave the house? Maura wanted to know if this sort of thing happened a lot and I didn't have any answers.

In a lot of ways, I know that I'm lucky. Maura didn't hesitate at all, clearing out her guestroom to make space for me. I wanted to convince myself that Maura insisted I move in with her because she was having a hard time with the separation, but she didn't need me as much as she knew I needed her. Even with Gracie taking up so much of her time, she still found a way to make me feel welcome. As much as I like that Maura named her daughter after her mother, I don't think I'll ever be able to hear that name without thinking of my Grace and how long it has been since she passed; in a lot of ways, it's easy to envy those moments when I don't know to miss her.

The worst part is that doubt becomes the most natural thing in the world. For a long time, Grace and I only really had one another. Even after Maura was born, there wasn't much outside of our family that I could count on except myself. Since Grace passed, I at least had myself; I had my body and my mind, but those were enough. My body is in as good a shape as a man ten years younger, but I… I sometimes wonder if I'm starting to slip away, if those parts of me that really matter will disappear and leave Maura looking after a stranger. Even in those moments when I feel confident in who I am, the doubt always finds a way to snap back into place.

"How do you like the campground, Dad?" Maura asks, as I unroll the tarp on the ground for my tent. With her and Gracie's tent up, Maura has moved over to starting the hamburgers.

"It's nice." I check over my shoulder to see Gracie coloring at the wooden picnic table near the fire pit, her red hair shining every time I look over. "It's a lot like where we used to camp when you were younger."

"Yeah, that's why I like coming here," Maura says, over the sizzle of hamburger patties on the portable grill. I wonder if she also likes coming here because this campground predated Steve, from when Maura and her friends would take trips up here during college. Maura had tried to take him camping early on into their marriage, but Steve never took to it. Maura only started to take the camping gear out of the attic after Steve had been living in his new house for a few months.

I've put so many tents together in my time that I don't even have to think about it as I snap the rods into place and slide them through the loops. This sort of thing had always come so naturally to me, but I have to focus myself on the bag of plastic tent spikes at my feet the whole time, even when my hands can practically assemble the tent on their own. I can tell that Maura holds herself back as she watches me put my tent together alone, but I've learned that my muscles still hang onto those memories that my mind would let float by. As I finish hammering the plastic spikes into the ground at the base of the tent, the burgers are ready to come off the grill. Maura has a bottle of water ready for me as I walk over.

"I want to sit next to Grandpa." Gracie says, as I take a long drink of water.

"You heard her, Dad." Maura smiles, placing a cheeseburger on a plate and sliding it my way.

"I'd love that, Sweetheart." I sit down next to Gracie, grabbing the mayonnaise for my hamburger. After a healthy amount of mayo, I place the bun on top of the cheeseburger and take a bite. "This is a great cheeseburger, honey."

"Thanks, Dad."

"What are we going to do now?" Gracie asks, taking a big bite of her burger.

"It's going to be getting pretty dark soon, but there are lots of things we could do tomorrow," Maura says, "Maybe we could go on a hike? There's a great little rock formation on the other side of the park, with a waterfall and everything. What do you think, Dad?"

"I'm not sure, Maura." Can she tell that I'm more tired than I want to be?

"Or we could look into canoeing? I think they rent them out by the lake."

"That sounds like fun." I lean over, kissing Gracie on the top of her head.

It starts to get dark not long after we finish dinner, and the tall trees make it feel like sunset lasts forever. We don't talk much as we clean the plates and make sure to hoist the cooler of food into a tree. It's a lot of work, but Maura and I manage to take care of everything while Gracie gets changed for bed. After we all brush our teeth at the campsite bathroom, I sit down near the fire and open a soda.

As Maura reads story after story, it's hard to not think about when she was Gracie's age. A lot of men seem to want a son, probably something to do with the idea of recreating yourself in the image of a younger man. For me though, I knew right away that there was something different about the relationship between fathers and daughters. Maybe it was only ever in my head, but I liked the idea of her thinking that she could always count on me.

When Maura leaves the tent, she makes sure to zip it all the way up and step quietly toward the picnic table for a beer. She sits down next to me on the bench.

"You've got a great kid there, Maura."

"Thanks, Dad." She opens the beer carefully, not making too much noise. The fire crackles and Maura doesn't say anything for a minute. "Dad, there's something that I wanted to talk to you about," she says, looking down at her beer. "About a few hours ago… you didn't just come looking for us at the rest stop, did you?"

"No, I didn't."

She stares at her beer. "How are you doing?"

"I'm alright, Maura."

"It's just that I could tell something was off, and I've noticed it a little more often lately. It makes me worry about the times I'm not noticing."

"I know you're worried, honey. We can't pretend that this isn't happening, but it isn't that bad yet."

"What has your doctor said?"

"It will get bad," I say, taking a drink of the soda, "maybe in a couple of years, maybe longer. He has me on some things to slow it down, but there's no stopping it."

"I've really enjoyed having you live with us these last months, but…" She stops.

"Are you getting tired of me, Maura?"

"No, Dad." She reaches over to place a hand on my arm. "You will always have a home with Grace and I, but will we always be able to give you the environment you need?"

"Maura, it's not that bad yet."

"I know, Dad, but what if we don't realize how bad it is until it's too late?"

I don't have an answer to that, and we both stare into the fire for a minute. Over the sounds of the fire, it's hard to tell if Gracie is asleep yet. "I'm still the same man I've always been, Maura. It's still me in here." I reach up and tap my temple, and she seems to believe me. There are days I wonder how much longer I'll be able to believe it myself.

"Grace and I love having you live with us, and it's made things easier for her since Steve moved out," Maura says, "you just know how I worry."

"I know. Just like your mom." She smiles when I say this, and it feels like we aren't going to say much more tonight. I stand up, drinking the last of my soda. "I think I'll turn in."

"Goodnight, Dad."

"Goodnight, honey." Walking to the 1-person tent, I unzip it and step inside. After I change and crawl into the sleeping bag, I look up at the tent as the air mattress shifts below my body. How many more good days do I have left in me?

I can tell I've started to lose a part of myself, but I hang onto the idea that there's still enough of me left to matter. I remember feeling so strong when I was a young man, feeling as though I could take care of Maura and Grace no matter what. I just want to keep feeling that.

IN THE MORNING I WAKE UP to the smell of cooking bacon. It takes me longer to get dressed than I would like, with the low tent ceiling bumping my head every time I try to move, but when I leave the tent I see that Maura and Gracie are already dressed and ready for whatever we decide to do.

"Good morning, Dad." Maura is at the portable stove, keeping a close eye on the bacon, while Gracie sits at the table with a new coloring book. "Did you sleep well?"

"I did, thanks."

"The bacon is about ready, and then I'll fry up the eggs. I also made coffee, if you'd like any." She grabs the cast iron griddle with a holder, as she turns off the burner.

"What's the plan for today?" I ask, sitting down next to Gracie.

"I was thinking about canoeing again," Maura says.

"It's been a long time for me, but I always did like the water." I pour myself some coffee into the blue camping mug as I turn to Gracie. "Your Grandma and I would go canoeing all the time when we first got married."

"I really want to go," Gracie says, as Maura starts cracking a handful of eggs into a metal bowl.

"What do you say, Dad? Maybe a calm little trip down the water?"

"I think it might be fun."

Set back from the water, the small rental shack has diagrams of the different river systems nearby and everything a potential renter would need to know about a canoe or raft. A group of college kids looks at the 4-person yellow rafts, one of them with a backpack slung over his shoulder. As they work to put on the bulky life vests, I notice the beer cans shining at the bottom of the open backpack. The four of them carry their raft off to the water, holding it by the neon yellow rope threaded a few times through the rings on the outside. They head upstream until I lose sight of them in the trees.

After Maura pays the man at the shack, we both examine the

diagram of all the rivers and streams. The main rivers are clearly marked, with recommendations for age and skill level. Though the two main rivers start from the same source, the map indicates where a fork to the right leads to a more exciting ride; the left fork would be too calm for rafting, but perfect for a short canoe trip. If Gracie were a little older and I were a little younger, maybe we could swap the canoe for a raft and follow the college kids. Instead, we gear up and start heading toward the launch point for the canoe.

We lift the canoe together, with Gracie following closely at Maura's side. It isn't that heavy, but I walk carefully to get to the edge of the water. The river is calm here and we slide the canoe into it. Once Maura is in the canoe, she and I help Gracie into the middle. I climb in at the stern of the canoe, and we use the paddles to shove into the middle of the river.

The water has some bumps here and there, but it remains largely calm as it winds through the forest. Maura and I paddle slowly through the water as she points out the different animals to Gracie.

After about fifteen minutes, we haven't seen or heard anyone else on the river. Dipping my paddle into the water, I start to hear several voices echoing toward us. As the river starts to pick up and bends, it's hard to tell exactly how far away the noise is.

"Maura?"

"Yeah, Dad?" In between paddling, she's pointing off somewhere in the distance for Gracie to look as the river bends again and blocks my view of the waterway behind us.

"Did you hear that noise?"

"No, I don't think so," Maura turns to look at me, but Gracie is still scanning the trees in the distance, "is everything ok?"

"Yeah, I just –" It feels foolish now, trying to say the words out loud. "It's probably nothing."

"Are you sure?" Maura says, scanning the woods around us. The water begins to ripple under the canoe, and we lurch forward suddenly. "Woah," Maura says, turning her gaze back in front of her, "it does look like it's getting a bit faster. Hold on, Grace."

As Maura and I paddle faster, I can hear the shouting more clearly without being able to tell where it is. I look behind us again, and see a glimpse of the yellow raft. Even though the raft is at least a hundred yards away, it's closer than it should be. The college kids are paddling much faster than they need to, and anyone who'd rafted before would know that that's just a good way to wear yourself out.

The water gets choppy, but Maura doesn't seem concerned until she sees up ahead where the river forks. The white-water bubbles to the top where the waterway splits off to the right, disappearing back to a leisurely flow further down on the left. As Maura looks ahead at where the water gets the choppiest, I keep my eyes on the raft each time I need to look behind myself to paddle. The college students are shouting and laughing, and I'd be willing to bet that there are more than a few empty cans on the floor of their raft.

"Maura, look at that raft," I say, as the raft continues to catch up. The college students are close, but the raft is further left than we are. "They're coming too fast."

"I see them, Dad." Maura tries to steer us closer to the shore, as we paddle against the choppy waters.

"Finally!" Someone from the raft shouts. It must have been a boring ride up to this point for them, but the rough water starts to carry their rubber raft much faster than our canoe. We're not too far from the split now, maybe another fifty yards.

As Maura tries to steer us to the left, the raft comes in quickly on our left side.

"Hey!" Maura shouts as she paddles. "You're on the wrong side."

"What?" One of the men on the raft shouts back. They are all paddling as hard as they can now, but this part of the river is too narrow for us to be side-by-side. When the front of their raft clips a submerged tree, the tail end flies into the canoe just as the waterway starts to split. I see a wall of yellow rush at me.

ALL I CAN SEE IS WATER, and I don't know how I got here. My arms and legs are moving on their own, until my head bursts out from the water. How did I get here? Where is Grace? Is she ok?

The water is moving quickly, and ahead of me I see a little girl pinned against a cluster of rocks. Her purple vest is the first thing I notice; if she's yelling for help, I can't hear anything above the noise of the river. The water pushes me closer to the edge of the riverbank, where I grab hold of a small tree stretching diagonally out from the shore.

I can't see anyone else, and my arms are already feeling heavy in the cold water. My life vest and the tree help, but the churning water moves so fast that it takes everything I have to keep my head at a safe distance above water. What is happening?

"Mommy! Grandpa!" I hear the little girl yell over the water, as I realize how tired I am. Why am I so tired? I look at my arms, and I don't know why they look so skinny. Why can't I pull myself up?

Even though the water is moving quickly, I can tell it's worse where the girl is. There's something familiar about her too, even from 50 yards away. Maybe it's her red hair, looking as brilliant as the first time I saw Grace. The top of the rock cluster pokes above the water's surface, but she is down in the water and pushed into a small groove of the cluster. The water swirls by her so quickly that when an overturned canoe gets close it slams against the other rocks before being sent quickly downstream. The girl is wedged in tight enough that her vest keeps her afloat, but the water is hitting too hard for her to stay there.

Without hesitating, I let go of the branch and let the river shove me downstream toward those rocks. It's even stronger than I would have thought, and the vest almost seems to be working against me as my arms slap at the water. As I get closer, I can hear the girl crying. I can barely see a flash of red hair, before my body slams into the rocks and it knocks the air out of me; the current and the vest manage to keep me from going under and luckily there are enough submerged rocks that I can get a foothold and barely manage to pull myself at least partially out of the water.

In the distance, I see a group of soaking wet college students appear on the shore along the side of the river. There's a woman who looks to be about my age with them, and she's running along the shore in our direction. I can tell from the look on her face that the woman is this girl's mother. She eyes the water between us and the shore; it can't be further than twenty feet, but she'd likely get herself killed if she tried to reach us. I crawl over the rocks, and the little girl looks up at me as I lift her to the top of the cluster. She says something, but the water is so loud it's hard to make out the words.

"It's ok," I yell above the rushing water, and I can feel her arms hugging around my neck. "I'm going to get you back to your mom, ok?" She nods, wiping at her eyes.

It's tempting to stay on the rocks and hope that help is on the way, but the water is hitting too hard. I don't know how much longer we'll be safe where we are. I look at the girl, who can't be more than six.

"We can't stay here!" I shout at the group on the shore.

"Are you ok?" The woman shouts back.

"We're ok, but we can't stay here!" I look at the five of them, all looking at me and the girl.

"Does anyone have a rope?" One of the men disappears for a few minutes and returns with a neon yellow rope.

The first time they toss the rope to me, I'm not fast enough and it falls into the water. On the second try, I manage to catch the rope and begin threading it through the little girl's life vest. I wish the water were calm enough that I could trust the idea of letting the people on shore drag us over one at a time, but it's easy to imagine how much damage the rocks and current would do before the rope could get the little girl to safety.

"We're going back in the river, and I need you to wrap your arms around my neck as tight as you can, ok?" I ask, over the noise of the water. "We're going to go together, and those people over there will pull us to shore.

She nods, but I can't imagine she's ever been this scared in her life.

"You must be pretty scared right now, huh?" She nods, shaking the tears from her eyes. "That's ok. I'm scared too, but that's why we need to be brave. I can tell you're brave. Do you want to know how I know?"

"How?"

"Your red hair. I've never met anyone braver than my Grace, and I think it's the red hair." I point to my head. "I don't have red hair, so I'll need you to be brave for both of us. Do you think you can help me?"

She nods.

"I know I can count on you." I stand up on the rock cluster, getting into a crouch. "We're going to get you back to your parents, but I need you to hold on as tight as you can. No matter what happens, will you keep hanging on?"

"I don't want to die," she says, crying again.

"It's ok, Sweetheart. That's not going to happen. I won't let anything happen to you." I turn my back to her, and I can feel her arms wrap tightly around my neck. I wrap the remaining slack of the rope loosely around my waist and look at the group on the shore. "Get ready!"

I notice the older woman at the front, holding the rope tightly. Lowering my body down into the water, I let go of the rock as soon as the water is up to my chin. If the girl says anything, I can't hear her over the sound of the water pushing us downstream and away from the rock cluster.

My arms and legs feel heavy as I swim for the shore, my body diagonally rushing down the river as I feel the girl's arms continue to squeeze tight. The swimming has more to do with getting away from the middle of the river than anything else, but I can feel the sharp tug of the rope on my waist. When my body hits a submerged rock, I feel a sharp pain in my side as my head goes under. The little girl screams, but she holds tighter as my body bounces off the rock and we continue to get pulled closer to the shore. I lift my head out of the water in time to see the girl's mother reaching out toward us as my head drops under the water again, but I manage to keep the little girl up. I can feel the rope being untied at the end and the little girl is taken off my back. I manage to keep my head up enough after the girl is safe, but it's hard to see anything other than the white water. Two of the college students rush forward as the rope is untied, reaching out to help lift me out of the water.

Once we're back on land, the girl is crying again as she hugs her mother. "It's ok," the woman says, "Dad, are you alright?"

I look around to see if there's anyone old enough to be this woman's dad, but I realize that she's looking at me. "What?" The little girl breaks away from her mom, and she's hugging my arm. I look down at the red head of hair, and I see Gracie looking up at me.

"I was brave, Grandpa."

"Yes, you were Sweetie." I look up at Maura, standing over Gracie and me.

"Are you alright, Dad?"

"Yeah." My whole body feels so sore. "Just a little banged up."

"Everyone in the raft and I were sent to the other side of the fork," Maura says, helping me to my feet. "Thank God you were here with us." Yeah, Thank God.

I look down at Gracie, and she's gripping my arm tight. When I kiss the top of her head, Gracie looks up at me just like her mother used to.

PATCHWORK

NOT LONG AFTER HE MOVED IN, Hank started with the den. He cut the carpet away in large swaths, stacking the loose strips of shag high in a corner of the room. When I got home from running errands, I found him staring at carpet swatches. It was a sign that his ribs were healing, so I didn't say anything. He didn't want to talk about the accident or things with Sara or how he now went out of his way to avoid driving by the preschool, so maybe not talking was best for all involved. I shrugged mostly to myself and tapped the ugliest swatch he had before heading to my room. Hank always had a knack for fixing things, and he embraced this at an early age. Growing up, there was never anything that he couldn't accomplish once he set himself on a path. If Hank needed a focus right now, what alternative was there? At least this path would keep him nearby.

Unlike my brother, I've never been much of a fixer. No, that gene passed right by me on the off chance that I wouldn't be an only child. Hank got a strong back and good hands, and I got whichever genes are necessary to stand awkwardly in the corner at a party and not mind a cupboard that doesn't quite close. When I first bought the house, Hank was probably the most vocally against it. I think he saw it only as a collection of repairs I would never make, but the trick is to not try to repair anything; instead, I like the random goulash of a house that results from previous owners fixing only that which could no longer be ignored. The house came with kitchen counters that dated back to the '60's and Living Room walls so faded that it was hard to tell which color they were meant to be, but this bothered everyone else a lot more than it bothered me. Even though the floorboards creaked and the orange-brown carpet in the den had a disconcerting sheen to it, both problems were more or less solved by not walking around barefoot. That approach suited me well when I lived alone.

Despite my own views of what constitutes immediate family, the single day of Bereavement Leave from work did little more than give me time to calculate out how much vacation I had saved up. In the days between the accident and the funeral, I really expected the funeral to be the hardest part for him. Hank barely reacted when the small coffin was lowered into the ground or when waves of people offered their condolences at the wake. He went through all the proper motions alongside Sara, but his eyes reflected the same focus that I had seen throughout our childhood every time he was about to take on something new. Once the funeral was over, Hank set himself on the task of closing almost every door in his life; he started with all of the friends who still had children, before moving onto Sara. It wasn't long until he succeeded in his goal, and my door was the only one that he still allowed to open.

On the Sunday before returning to work, I settle out onto the porch. After hammering new strips of wood into whatever's left after you pull up old carpet and pound new carpet into place, Hank's next project was painting. The thick scent of new paint in the Living Room mixes well with the smell of fresh carpet, resulting in a collection of fumes effectively driving me to the outskirts of my property. I try not to dwell on the fact that my house is being remade in my brother's image, instead I have begun spending my evenings rocking on the old porch swing that came with the house – the soft creaking of old wood and metal chain hasn't caught Hank's attention just yet. As Hank undoubtedly sets himself on a new project, I gather forms and papers around me on the porch. When Hank's recently forwarded mail started lying open and forgotten on the kitchen table, I wanted to make sure that the necessary stuff was still taken care of. He muttered his permission for me to work through it all, before returning to his projects. Insurance forms and legal letters gather around my feet, while I set aside only those items that can't move forward without Hank.

At the top of the stack of open mail is a new letter from Hank's life insurance company, requesting a copy of the accident report in order to close things down on their end. Turning slightly, I catch movement out of the corner of my eye. A small orange leaf floats down, landing on the copies of the death certificate piled next to me. Over the last three weeks, I barely noticed the changing weather. The numerous pamphlets that lay stacked on the top of my dresser, inside the glovebox of my car, and in the inside pocket of my jacket warn against ignoring changes at a time like this. None of them seemed to acknowledge that change was happening beyond anyone's power to stop it. The status of Hank and Sara's marriage had changed abruptly, and his employment status was changed to whatever best fit this particular need for time off. A lot of things had been changing, so when were the warning sirens meant to start?

With so many forms requiring the report, it can be hard to keep my mind from returning to the accident every time I read through it. It's pretty straight forward as far as reports go, mechanically detailing the events of the accident. Between the accident report and the death certificate, it's all clear enough that no one needs anything from Hank that can't be found in one document or the other. The driver who hit Hank died on impact, so maybe the insurance companies just don't see a point in pursuing it any further. No one has needed to talk to me, and I can only guess that it's the same for Sara. She had received the call from the first policeman on the scene, but I was her first call right after. I didn't know what the rules are in that kind of situation, so I found myself walking around Hank's car not even sure what I should be looking for. Glass was scattered around the cement, and the plaster from the nearby building had sprinkled the roof of Hank's car. The back-passenger side door was crumpled into the front of the building, where metal gave way to brick.

None of the insurance companies dive into the minutiae that sticks out in my mind, and none of the forms need anything more than the facts. They don't need to know that sometimes it can be surprising what kids latch onto. She always had lots of toys, but Emily really liked the small sock monkey that I gave her as a last-minute gift on my way to some occasion or another. The paperwork didn't need to know how much Emily enjoyed spinning that sock monkey around by its flimsy tail, and how she used to laugh as it twirled through the air. The forms gathered at my feet don't have a box for me to put the one thing that dominates my thoughts every time I reach for a copy of the accident report: the sight of a small sock monkey resting on a car seat stained red.

When I pull myself back out of that memory, I notice that it's starting to get dark. After I gather up all the forms from the porch and head inside, I pause at the door to the basement. In Hank's newly annexed workshop, an electric sander buzzes. The sanding will likely persist well into the evening hours. It's been like this every night, and I sometimes wonder if Hank sleeps at all. Once the sanding is done, Hank will be on the lookout for other noise to add to the house. Every ounce of oomph that our family tree has to offer can be seen in his eyes, and it's always been like this; it's the kind of drive that makes it hard to sit still sometimes. There will always be more for him to do, and no reason good enough to stop. That difference felt so excessive when we were younger, as though Hank had been born already a hundred yards closer to some finish line that I couldn't quite see. We both carried that distance into adulthood, and I watched as it developed into a cordial detachment interrupted only by major holidays and birthdays. Distance always came naturally for my relationship with Hank, so I never put in much effort to make it any other way. That all ended roughly three weeks ago.

Hank is already awake by the time I leave for work in the morning, the sound of an electric drill humming from the basement. Three weeks feels like a long time if it's spent on a beach somewhere, but the only big thing waiting for me at work is a condolence card signed by more than a few people I wouldn't be able pick out of a crowd. Most of my coworkers give me a wide berth around the office, leaving me to sort through a collection of backlogged emails. If Hank notices I'm not around, there's no indication of it. As I read through one outdated email after another, I can't help wondering if this was how things started for Sara and everyone else. If Hank decides he needs to start shutting me out, what happens after that? Every few minutes throughout the day, I look at my phone as it lies silent on my desk.

By the time I get home, several orange leaves are gathered on the porch swing. As I bend down to brush the leaves off, I notice that the wood of the swing is no longer weather-beaten and faded; when I give it a push, the familiar creak is gone. I can't help sighing as I enter through the door, pausing at the silence that greets me. At first, it feels like I'm living alone again. After a moment, I hear the shuffling of feet and gentle humming of cardboard scraping against hardwood upstairs. Passing the new cabinets and updated countertops in the kitchen, I walk up the stairs. The absence of creaky floorboards makes it hard to announce my presence, but I do my best; my efforts to step loudly on the carpet upstairs also turn out to be pointless.

Ever since Hank moved in, the boxes have been packed away in the spare room. It got to be too hard for Sara to keep looking at them, especially with Hank gone; so the boxes came here soon after Hank did. Pictures, clothes, and toys all confined to cardboard limbo while Hank focused on fixing things that didn't look so broken to me. Approaching the room, I find him holding a picture frame. Hank's eyes stay locked on the frame, even though I can tell he knows I'm here.

"Hey buddy," I say, standing in the doorway. This is the first time he's been in here, since the boxes were moved in. "What are you up to?"

Hank doesn't look up. "I've been thinking about what to do with this stuff."

"Yeah?" From where I'm standing, I can see a picture of Hank and Emily at some museum. Hank's eyes are locked on the faces that look back at him.

"Everything's been up here, just sitting. I don't think I need to hang onto all this." His words are firm and matter-of-fact. "I think it all needs to go."

"Alright, so where—" The sound of the picture frame hitting the hardwood floor startles me, and I watch as small pieces of the frame break off. The glass inside the frame cracks, with fragments tearing into the picture. After a slight pause, another picture frame is pulled from the box and thrown to the ground without much in the way of ceremony.

"Hank, are you sure—" Crash. Crash. Crash. Soon the floor has a collection of broken glass and fractured frames. Wood splinters and glass shards begin to gather around Hank's feet.

"None of it matters." Hank grabs a souvenir plate from a family trip to Michigan, allowing it to fall to the ground with another crash. "What good is any of this anyways?"

When the first box is empty, Hank throws it to the side. Moving to the next box, he tears off the tape and begins to dig through. He picks up a small ornament that he'd purchased when they first learned that Sara was pregnant. Three ceramic dogs smile up at Hank, a nuclear family in canine form. After the ornament breaks against the floor, ceramic shards spread out across the room.

"Are you sure you don't want to hang onto any of this?" I take a few steps into the room, my shoe crunching down on small pieces of wood and glass.

"It's all just useless trinkets we don't need." I watch as he throws more store-bought keepsakes against the floor.

"What about the memories?"

Hank stops for a moment, his eyes focused downward into the box. When I take another step forward, I see that there's only one thing left. It's another picture frame, but it stands out from the debris scattered across the floor. The Popsicle sticks of the frame display random spots of glue and paint, evidence of less-than-skilled labor at work. The picture inside the frame looks like a first draft; Hank and Emily are sitting on a bench with their attention focused off in the distance, well beyond whoever took the photo. When Sara first started helping her make the frame for Hank, this was the picture that Emily had insisted on. I asked Emily once why she liked the picture so much, and she just said that she liked how silly it was. In Sara's colorful, feminine handwriting the word "Daddy" runs along the bottom of the frame. He stands firm and solid in front of the box, his hands stopping just short of reaching inside.

"Emily and I were driving around one day, probably out running errands. She must have been around three and a half at the time. I was driving, and we weren't really doing anything special. Randomly, she starts singing a song just for me. It's hard to describe, but I remember feeling so happy at that moment as I listened to her serenade me for no reason. It was one of those things that just doesn't happen much—something spontaneous and organic. A moment that you try to hang onto for as long as you can, and now I can't even remember which song it was." Hank pauses for a moment. "I've been waking up for weeks with that song in my head, and now one of my favorite memories is starting to fall apart. It's like I'm losing her all over again."

When Hank picks up the picture frame, I step forward again and place a hand on his shoulder. "Why don't you let me hang onto this one for now?"

"Just leave me alone, Daniel." Hank says, shrugging off my hand.

"I don't think that's a good idea," I say softly. He doesn't respond, instead raising the frame up slowly.

Even as I reach for the frame, it feels like a mistake. It's not the sort of thing I should be doing, but that doesn't stop me. When I have a grip on the frame, I pull. Hank pulls back, not quite wrenching it away. I don't know if he means to or not, and it doesn't really matter; I just feel Hank's left hand hit me hard in the chest, and my fingers lose contact with the Popsicle sticks. Falling back, I can feel the ceramic debris under my shoe for just a moment before it gives way underneath me and I lose my footing.

When my head hits the wall, I see a flash of white behind my eyelids. By the time I realize that I had been falling, my body is already settled on the ground. I pull myself up to sitting, my back leaning against the wall. The room isn't spinning exactly, but I'm not in any hurry to stand up. This fight is pretty representative of our childhood, with Hank usually winning once the age difference stopped doing me much good. Hank looks down at me, his face an uneasy mix of guilt and anger. His breathing is quick from the burst of adrenalin, but I watch his face soften as he registers what just happened.

"Are you alright?" Hank asks, after a few seconds.

"Yeah, probably."

Slowly, Hank slides down the wall to sit next to me. He still holds the handmade picture frame, staring at it.

"I keep rolling it over in my mind. All the time. I saw the other car at the last moment, just enough time to react. I didn't even think about it, not at all – when I saw the other car, I turned the steering wheel just enough so it would hit the driver side as much as possible. I should've gotten a lot worse than some broken ribs, but there wasn't any hesitation. Maybe I thought that would help keep her safe somehow if I could take the brunt of the hit." Hank sighs, looking at the frame. "I hadn't thought about that building with the brick, and now it's just me here."

I can feel one of the pamphlets in my inside jacket pocket, the slight weight of it just enough to notice on most days. I've read the pamphlet more times than I can count. It has a list of resources to consult–phone numbers and websites laid out clearly, some of them even focused on losing a child. I can picture the large block font, but I don't reach for it.

"What are we supposed to do when our instinct turns out to be so wrong?" Hank asks softly. He runs a finger across the word at the bottom of the frame. "I just don't know how to fix this."

"Maybe that's alright for now," I say, lifting my hand to rest on Hank's shoulder.

The tools downstairs are silent and the paint continues to dry, while the sound of Hank's grief spreads throughout the house. Hank's body shakes as he cries for what might be the first time since the accident, heavy tears falling on the Popsicle stick frame. Amidst the piles of broken memories, Hank doesn't need me to say anything else. He'll eventually insist that we get up and sweep away the debris around us, but that can wait. Trying to fix it all can wait.

DROUGHT CONDITIONS

IN THE LAST SIX MONTHS, a steady routine had developed for Peter. He'd been fortunate to land a workstation not too far from the time clock, so he could typically count on beating the others to it when the 6 am bell rang. While the line continued to form around the timeclock, Peter could make it to the soap station and peel the night's grease off his bright red arm hairs before making it to his car. On the good days, his truck could slip out of the steel works plant parking lot before most of the others had made it to their cars. With the plant about 10 miles out of town, his morning drive gave him a full tour of the town he'd known most of his life.

Harrison was the kind of place that felt like it didn't belong in California, so removed from the image of the state that seemed to draw in others from around the world. It was little more than a speed bump for anyone heading to the vineyards or beaches, leaving the outdated buildings and drought conditions for the locals. With its yellowed lawns and faded house paint, Harrison was a town without much to boast about. The houses clumped together in over-packed subdivisions, until the town itself abruptly gave way to dirt and weeds on roads that ran alongside the highway. Occasional buildings would line the road outside of town, serving as little more than ellipses on the grey-brown dirt. Where the town limits appeared to be littered with yellowed overgrowth, the sides of the old highway were overrun. Long stretches of road held little more than the promise of civilization in the distance. Peter would watch the town dissolve into nothing each night as he drove to the plant, reversing the process again in the morning. With the sun fully starting to rise, Peter left the music off and started to think.

He'd think about his mother's grave, and how he hoped she liked it. He'd think about how out of everyone he'd known and been related to, only his uncle Paul had come through for him six months ago. He'd think about the two years since he'd seen his father or stepmother, now ex-stepmother. He'd sometimes think about his former stepsister Claire, still picturing the awkward twelve-year-old he'd last seen as he hastily packed the few things his dad would let him take into the old truck. He pictured his dad watching from the porch, arms folded while an unseen timer clicked down; he'd been given an hour to get out of there and never return. Peter saw Claire peeking through the living room blinds to watch him before a hand snatched her away from the window. But mostly Peter would think of Simon as he pulled into the driveway of his uncle Paul's house and slipped in through the side door of the garage. The house was normally starting to wake up by the time Peter entered the garage, sliding into bed while it started to warm up outside and laying on top of the sheets that always seemed to smell of Simon for days after his visits. It had started to warm up as the calendar moved into July, but he could normally count on at least four good hours of sleep until the heat radiating off of the garage door would eventually stir him.

The sleep was normally hazy if it lasted past that fourth hour, disturbed by the growing California heat to a point where it felt only slightly better than not sleeping at all. Just as Peter could feel the garage heat overpowering the industrial fan in the corner of his makeshift bedroom, the phone cut through what little sleep was left. Looking over, Peter saw that it was Simon. He couldn't remember a time when Simon had called this early, normally calling late on Peter's nights off or knocking on the garage's side door after a double shift. Simon's lithe frame liked to appear in the doorway of that side door late at night, confident that no one inside the house would notice. Not that either of them thought Paul or his roommates would care, but they knew Simon would.

"I don't have anyone else to call." Simon's voice carried through the phone, the sound of traffic behind him. Peter's mind was still foggy from a dreamless sleep, and he shook his head a bit to focus. "My car started to overheat, and I had to pull over."

"Where are you?" Peter rolled over to look at his watch on the bedside table. It was about 10:30, and the house would be thankfully empty by now.

"I'm on the side of the highway. I can see the Fulkerth Avenue exit, but there's nothing around for miles." Today was meant to be another in a long line of triple digit days.

"I can be there in 10 minutes." Peter scanned the floor for his pants.

"Thanks."

Peter pulled on his pants and grabbed a t-shirt from the armoire against the wall, trying to smooth down his ruffage of red hair before leaving the garage to enter the kitchen. He rummaged through the trash, grabbing an old 2-liter bottle that had not yet been thrown in with the rest of the recycling. As the 2-liter bottle filled with warm tap water, Peter grabbed a few bottles of water from the refrigerator. With his shoes on and an armful of water bottles, Peter slipped out of the side door of the garage.

As long as his windows stayed rolled all the way down, the heat in Peter's old truck was at least manageable. In the absence of working AC, the few bottles of water were the only source of cold in the truck; they rattled around the floor of the passenger side, banging into the 2-liter bottle that lay on top of an old rag.

Peter saw Simon on the side of the highway, standing away from the hot metal of the old sedan. With the summer heat pressing on relentlessly, a grey haze colored the horizon in all directions. The warm breeze had left Simon covered in a mixture of sweat and dirt, his sandy blonde hair looking washed out in the harsh sun. Peter pulled his truck up behind Simon's car, stepping out as the traffic streamed by them. There was a moment of visible relief before Simon seemed to catch himself, setting his face in the same stoic look that Peter remembered from that night in church all those years ago.

"I thought you'd need this." Peter tossed Simon one of the cold bottles of water as he got out of his truck. Catching the bottle with one hand, Simon wiped his brow with the back of his arm. He drank the water without hesitation, while Peter reached back inside his truck for the 2-liter bottle and the rag. Walking to the front of Simon's car with the bottle, Peter placed his hand close to the engine; it was too hot to touch but felt cool enough to not risk damaging anything.

"Turn it on and keep it in park, while I add in the water." Peter said, removing the radiator cap with the old rag. When the engine started, Peter slowly poured in the warm water. With the radiator cap back on and the empty 2-liter in hand, he walked to Simon's rolled-down driver's side window. "You're probably alright to get home if you take it easy, but I'll follow you." Simon nodded, his forehead already covered again with sweat.

The sun highlighted the patches of rust on Simon's car as they drove back into town. The boxy sedan looked like any number of models that Peter had seen in his life, the faded beige paint matching the endless expanse of weeds they drove by. Any official markings had fallen off it long ago, with only the letters 'o' and 'l' still hanging to the back of the car. Peter held his breath every time Simon stopped at a red light, thankful when the car lurched forward without overheating again. By the time Simon parked in front of his house, Peter was already reaching for another bottle of cold water. He expected Simon to curse or yell or tell Peter to drive away before anyone saw him, but he didn't; taking a moment, Simon just looked at the patch of weeds in front of the house and sighed. It had been a garden once, but these days Simon's dad only planted a wide variety of beer bottles and cigarette butts. Simon walked over to the truck, leaning on the passenger-side door.

"Can we go for a drive?" Simon asked.

"Are you sure you don't want to go inside and cool off?"

Simon looked at his dad's car in the driveway, one taillight broken from a run-in with a trash can four months ago. "I just need a break, Peter."

Simon opened the passenger-side door of the truck and climbed in. Peter drove off without any more questions, eventually parking behind an abandoned department store. A small breeze began to kick up as Peter turned off his truck.

"We're going to be stuck here forever," Simon said after a moment, lighting a cigarette as he got out of the cab and pulled down the tailgate to sit.

"You really think so?" Peter asked, sitting beside him. Peter wondered how much taller he looked sitting next to Simon, Peter's broad shoulders and six-foot-frame seeming to accentuate everything compact about Simon. Even when they'd first met, Peter towered over him. Having hit puberty at an early age, it was only in recent years that some of the kids he towered over in youth group had begun to catch up. Simon remained about six inches shorter than Peter.

"No one ever gets out of here." It wasn't entirely true but wasn't entirely false either. There weren't a lot of good options to be found, but bad choices were in ample supply. Patterns have a way of turning into gospel, and it was clear that Simon couldn't shake it from his mind. "Besides, the few who do leave always wind up back here eventually. You're a pretty good example of that." Simon looked away after he said it.

Peter had been living in Sacramento with his mother when she started to get sick. Even before turning eighteen, Peter had been able to find a handful of jobs in the years after he left Harrison – never anything glamorous, but enough to help his mom out with the steadily increasing rent. He'd never been one for school, but had found a way to get that diploma as his interests steadily shifted more toward his after-school work. It only took a few really bad test results to change the balance he and his mom had found, and the money Peter made shifted from saving for trade school to keeping their heads above water with the hospital bills. Peter's mother had fought hard and long, with nothing to show for it but a pile of bills that continued to trickle in after she passed. His mother's insurance managed to cover most of the expenses after she was gone, but it still left Peter without enough to afford living on his own.

There hadn't been enough options in Sacramento to keep him there, and luckily Paul had been able to make room in his garage; Paul's three roommates hadn't initially been happy about losing the garage, but they seemed to care more about the extra $600 a month that Peter had offered to split amongst the three of them. Even though Paul owned the house, Peter knew that the mortgage was too high to afford without roommates; Peter tried to make himself scarce when he could, to make it easier on everyone. The two years in Sacramento had gone by with only a handful of texts from Simon, and then one day he saw Simon again at the store and it all came back. After Simon slipped a hastily written phone number into Peter's hands on his way to the frozen foods, that next night off was the first time Simon had come over to the garage. Their time was stolen either late at night or in the privacy behind that metal door, Simon normally so paranoid of being seen by someone from church. It was nice to sit so close together out in the open, even if only one of them was really out. It had been about three months, and this might have only been the second time they'd been outside while the sun was up.

"What brought this up? Is it about the car?" Peter asked.

"No, it's not just the car. It's everything. I had been on the way back from Modesto to go to the mall, and this shit happens. That's what I get for wanting new jeans."

"You're ok though, right?" Sitting on the hard metal tailgate, it still felt good being close to him. His time with Simon was the only time Peter didn't think about their history, the smell and touch of him at least temporarily freeing Peter from the complexities of their time together.

"I was standing in front of my car at the side of the highway after I called you, and I just found myself wondering 'What the fuck am I doing?' I always thought I'd find a way to go to college and move out and a million other things. Like, is this really the best I can hope for? Leaning on you more and more, and just waiting for the next big thing to break down or fall apart?"

There was a slow monotony of things in Harrison, and it looked to be bearing down on Simon. "Have things gotten worse than usual though?"

"I don't know," Simon sighed. "I turn nineteen next week."

"I remembered. I was going to ask if you had plans."

"I don't, but that's not why I brought it up." Simon's eyes were fixed on the dirty grey wall in front of them that separated the parking lot from a subdivision of houses. "It just all feels so pointless staying here, but I'm also not sure how to get out. Army or college seems to be the only way, and neither of those panned out. I can't keep putting off getting my life together and expect it'll actually happen." Simon sighed, possibly thinking about how even his flat feet had conspired to keep him in Harrison.

"We aren't really trapped here. It just feels that way: perception vs. reality," Peter said.

"If that's how it feels, then what difference does it make?" Simon asked, maybe knowing there wouldn't be an answer. "At a certain point, any difference between perception and reality is purely academic."

"So, we're all screwed then?" Peter asked.

"Afraid so."

"Let's leave then."

"Yeah," Simon scoffed, putting his cigarette out on the metal bed of the truck.

"Really," Peter said, looking at Simon now. "Let's get out of here and see what happens."

"You mean it?" Simon asked, as though this single idea could not have appeared without Peter's help.

"All of this is definitely in your head, but maybe a change of scenery would be good for you."

"Where would we go?"

"Does it matter? Isn't anywhere better than here?"

"Yeah," Simon said, "but what about Paul?" In their lighter moments, Simon sometimes liked to joke about the way Peter probably enjoyed living in his uncle's house surrounded by men. The faux-jealousy implied by the joke always seemed to ignore the fact that, despite whatever their feelings might be for one another, Peter expected that Simon would never admit to having a boyfriend as long as he lived in Harrison. He still went to the church that would no longer have Peter and must still feel some relief that when Peter's dad caught them kissing after youth group that Simon had gotten away without being identified.

"Paul's a good guy, but he'll probably be relieved to get the garage back and stop having to fight with the roommates about it." In the months since he'd settled at the steel works plant, the urgency that had driven Peter back to Harrison began to fade. The bills had started to cease, and he no longer lived in constant worry of overdraft fees. "Besides, there's not much here that I can't find somewhere else."

Simon watched his feet dangle off the side of the truck bed. Peter didn't ask about Simon's dad. Simon's dad was too much like Peter's, sharing all of the same faults and flaws that caused Simon to sneak around late at night.

"I have a little bit of money saved up, but enough to get things going." Peter enjoyed being able to start putting some money away, without first running through a pile of medical bills to pay. "Do you have anything?"

"A few hundred, but I can sell my car." There was the hint of excitement in Simon's eyes now. "Would this thing make the trip?" He patted the tailgate with his hand.

Peter had recently replaced the engine and bought new tires, even though it would have made more sense for him to sell the truck for parts and get something else. The old pickup would surely outlive them both, but it needed someone like Peter to care enough to keep it out of the junkyard for a while longer.

"I'm not worried," Peter said, "But won't that punch a hole in your theory? If we can leave in a few days, couldn't we just leave at any point?"

"Maybe we need to leave together. Ride each other's coattails to freedom."

"You really are pretty crazy."

"I always thought that's what you liked about me." Simon pressed closer to him, his arm brushing against Peter. "When do you have to be at the plant?"

"Not until ten." Peter looked at his watch. It wasn't even noon yet.

"I think my car should cool off a bit more. Want to kill some time before you drop me off again?" Simon asked.

"What did you have in mind?" Peter asked, stifling a yawn.

Simon looked around the empty parking lot. "How about we go back to your place?"

"I should probably get some sleep, but I can call you tomorrow morning after I get off work."

"I wouldn't mind a little sleep."

"You're actually going to sleep over?" Peter asked. In the last few months since they'd reconnected, Simon always managed to find one reason or another to avoid sleeping over until Peter had stopped offering. It was like whichever fantasy Simon put together in his head quickly started to dissolve right after sex.

"You know, you could kick me out afterward if you didn't want me to stay."

"Never said I was going to. I just need to reevaluate how I see the world, with this new bit of information forced on me."

"Shut up." Simon jumped off the tailgate. Peter smiled as they drove back to the garage.

When Peter woke up later in the day, he was surprised to feel Simon still next to him in bed and began the careful process of extracting his arm from under him. Looking at his clock, he saw it was only half past four. By the time Peter got out of the shower, Simon was stirring from his nap. He still lay in bed, propping himself up as Peter walked out of the bathroom.

"You're looking pretty happy." Peter pulled on his pants for what felt like the tenth time that day.

"That was nice," Simon smiled, "but you don't have to follow through with any of what we said before. Not if you don't want to."

"I want to," he said, bending down to give Simon a kiss. "When do you want to leave?"

"How about tomorrow?" Simon asked. "It'll give me some time to get rid of my car and square a few things away. Sound doable?"

"Alright. I'll tell them tonight that it will be my last day." The thought of giving his notice at work made Peter happier than he expected. "Should you be heading off to work pretty soon?"

"I don't have to." Simon smiled at Peter again. Peter knew Simon's schedule as well as his own, but the look in Simon's eyes was asking a question. He could trace it all back to that smile, making him plunge headfirst into what almost anyone would have considered a bad idea. Before that first kiss, first time, and first heartbreak, that smile had a way of making Peter forget that he should know better.

"You know, I could be a little late to work." Simon looked around, taking in the unfinished walls and large metal door. "I might actually miss this garage." This was very much a lie.

IT HAD NEVER BEEN PETER'S IDEA to go to church in the first place. This was something that his father had always insisted upon, along with youth group. It had started in order to keep Peter out of the way while his dad went to the singles group, continuing so that his dad and new stepmom could go through the phases of the honeymoon period. Even from that first youth group meeting, Peter felt different from everyone else. It wasn't just that some of them came from families so strict in their beliefs that they weren't allowed to celebrate Halloween, that Peter already knew he wasn't interested in sneaking off with one of the girls to make out while the youth pastor went to check on the younger kids, or even that most of the time during silent prayer Peter just sat there wondering what his mom was doing. The ways in which Peter felt different from everyone else in youth group seemed too numerous to count, increasing by one the moment that Simon joined their ranks.

Peter had long been volunteering with the younger kids by this point, seizing on any excuse to get away from his peers as they found creative new places to make out. Peter was happiest spending time with his stepsister and the other children. Peter had still been required to attend the first half of youth group with the other teenagers, sometimes catching a look from Simon that made him wonder why Simon had quickly built a reputation for making out with different girls each week. When their friendship began, Peter had been sure that it was all in his head. As they would hang out after school or go to the movies together, Simon's constant talk of girls had Peter convinced that it would only ever be a fantasy. And then one day, they'd both gone in the same direction when they tried to pass each other in Simon's living room. When they bumped into one another, Simon hadn't taken a step back like Peter did. Simon hadn't held his hands up in apology like Peter did, and instead stepped closer until Peter could feel Simon reach out toward him. That first time they kissed in Simon's empty house, Peter felt things click into place for just a moment. Simon might not have been the first boy Peter thought about kissing, but his were the first lips that Peter had touched. Over the next several months things progressed quickly in the hours before Simon's parents came home from work, and Peter would try to not think about how Simon could spend hours in bed with him and then hold hands with a girl later that day in youth group.

It probably shouldn't have happened at all, except that Peter had needed to get some supplies for the pastor's wife and Simon had made an excuse to step away from the two girls who wanted to know why he wouldn't choose between them. Peter couldn't even remember why they had decided to take the risk during youth group, especially when their routine in the hours after school had felt so safe. But they were there in the hallway of the church, kissing as though nothing mattered. And then Peter's dad was there and Simon was running out of a side door into the night. When Peter's dad dragged him in front of the pastor to confess his sin, Simon had reappeared to join the group close enough to hear everything. When Peter refused to name the other misguided youth in the incident, Simon refused to make eye contact with him. While the church didn't officially kick him out, it was still an excommunication; no one wanted to admit that it was happening. The refusal to apologize or try to change or pretend like his father had seen anything other than an inescapable truth finally gave Peter what his dad had always denied: freedom to live in Sacramento.

For the most part, Paul was the only family member aside from Peter's mom who kept in contact. Paul had never bought into religion the way the rest of Peter's family had, instead shrugging when Peter finally told him why he would be moving to Sacramento. Simon had kept in contact for a while, maybe out of guilt mixed with something more. These messages came late at night, when Peter suspected that the rest of Simon's family was already asleep. The texts became less frequent until they stopped altogether, and Peter started to see all of the public Facebook posts of Simon and his girlfriend from church. Peter never tried to call his dad from Sacramento, knowing that he'd receive only a dial tone after announcing himself. He didn't have any desire to reconnect anyways, certain that his dad would never accept the man Peter could feel himself becoming. Even when Peter moved back to Harrison, he knew that any chance encounter with his dad at a store or around town would result in his dad pretending to see a stranger when he looked in Peter's direction.

GIVING HIS NOTICE WENT THE WAY PETER EXPECTED, his supervisor just shrugging in general irritation as Peter went to his machine to begin cutting steel plates. He grabbed a long bar of metal and fed it into place, as the machines around the plant droned on loudly. The long nights were hard at first, and often made the hours seem much longer than they already were. With various pieces of machinery around the plant whirring loudly at all times of the day, it was easy to not think much of anything. Even the major injuries were often considered more of a joke than anything else, especially since the old veterans liked to believe that accidents only happen to those who deserve them. Peter's hands bore a few scars from cuts of different severity, but he usually put thoughts of anything worse out of his mind.

Worse than the threat of injury was the other risk of working here. The atmosphere of the place could be stifling without anything for you beyond these walls. It was hard not to think about that, with the afternoon's conversation fresh in his mind. As the hours ticked by, Peter filled the barrel next to his machine with freshly cut metal plates as his thoughts stretched far and wide to wherever he could find himself in a week. The thought of never seeing this place again was enough to make him barely notice that the hours were ticking by quicker than usual. When the leaving bell rang, Peter left through the large metal entryway of the plant without even stopping to wash up. Once he got home, the garage felt a little cooler than it had been. Peter was asleep not long after his shower had washed away the night's grime.

It wasn't much of a surprise when he heard the side door of the garage open and felt Simon crawl into bed beside him. On those days the heat wouldn't stir him, Simon would wake him up after finishing the first half of a split shift. Peter could set his watch by when Simon finished work on Friday afternoons. The smell of stale coffee and cooking oil clung to him, even after Simon left his uniform in a pile on the garage floor.

"So, are you still onboard for this half-baked idea of ours? Didn't smarten up, did you?"

Peter opened his eyes slowly, shifting to face Simon. "I've never been that smart to begin with."

"Good, I like you cute and dumb. Have you thought about where you'd like us to go first?" Simon asked.

"I haven't really thought about it."

"How would you feel about going through Idaho and Wyoming? I'd like to explore those states for a little while."

"Do the people who live in Idaho and Wyoming even want to explore those states?" Of all the first stops that Simon could have proposed, Peter couldn't see the appeal of a couple of flyover states.

"We went there once, when I was younger. I think the plan had been to focus mostly on Yellowstone, but my mom liked exploring the random other bits of the states. I liked the brick buildings that you don't really see out here, and my dad kept talking about how cheap the gas was every time we stopped."

"That sounds nice."

"Yeah," Simon smiled, "Before my mom got sick and before my dad started drinking, we used to talk about going back to the park and exploring more of Wyoming. I don't really remember too much of that trip, but I have this image in my head of green fields that seemed to stretch on forever." Even though everyone liked to think of California as a liberal behemoth, the reality was that Harrison had always been a dark red spot in that sea of blue; Wyoming might not be that different from what Peter had already learned to live with.

"Would you want to stick around there for a bit?"

"I don't know," Simon shrugged, "I could find a job waiting tables pretty much anywhere, so maybe Wyoming could be alright. I like the idea of being able to see lots of blue sky during the day and endless stars at night. Do you think you could be happy in a flyover state?"

"I think I could be happy in a lot of places," Peter wrapped his arm around Simon, "If you want to try Wyoming, then let's give it a shot. If it's good, then we stay for a while; if it's just as bad as here, then we find another random spot on the map and start driving." He laid back on the bed, fixing his gaze at the ceiling. "Any other plans I should probably know about?"

"A garden," Simon said without hesitation, "anywhere we end up, I'd like to get a garden going. Maybe it wouldn't be so bad to grow something for once." Peter remembered a picture of Simon's mom on the mantle from years ago: she stood by a beautiful garden in front of their house, smiling proudly.

"For what it's worth, I think you'd be good at gardening," Peter said. Simon didn't say anything at first, but his body moved closer into Peter.

"I gave my notice, but I have to work the dinner shift. We can't leave until sometime later tonight. Does that work for you?"

"Cutting it a little close." Peter laughed, or at least tried to laugh; it ended up coming out as more of a yawn.

"Shut up. We leave later tonight, and we'll be fine. Just pick me up from work at seven. Alright?"

"Alright. You'll have everything settled by then?"

"Yeah. Even got my cousin to buy my car off me." Peter wanted to ask if Simon had told his dad or anyone from church, but he knew that Simon wouldn't explain the real reason he was leaving. There might be no explanation at all, just a note left on his way to work. Simon had chosen them over Peter once before, and maybe it would be better if Simon left without having to make a choice again.

"Glad that you're still feeling good about all of this."

"I am."

"I should probably get up now and try to make use of the day." Peter started to get up, but he felt Simon's hand on his arm.

"Go back to sleep, you still look tired."

"I didn't set my alarm. Don't want to oversleep."

"Don't worry, I'll wake you up." Peter almost argued, but instead just put his arm around Simon and laid his head back down on the pillow. When Peter pulled Simon's body into his, it was nice to not feel him pull away. It didn't take long for Peter to fall asleep, with images of expansive green fields in his dreams.

NOT LONG AFTER SIMON WOKE PETER UP, he had to leave to get back for his dinner shift. While Peter lay in bed wondering whether he should set his alarm and try for more sleep, he could hear his uncle's truck pull into the driveway. Peter pulled on pants and made his way into the kitchen, just as his uncle was setting the mail on the counter.

"Morning," Paul said wryly, as Peter got water from the refrigerator. "How was work?"

"Never anything exciting." Paul had worked on road crews for most of his working life; at 55, Paul was in better shape than most people Peter's age. "It's at least better than the alternative."

"Not too bad with the heat?" Peter asked.

"Nah." Paul opened the refrigerator and pulled out a bottle of Gatorade. "If one of us gets heat stroke, it messes up their whole bottom line. They watch that shit pretty close, so it's been a lot of off–brand sports drinks and mandatory breaks in the shade."

"Hey Paul—" Peter started, "I think I've gotta get out of here for a bit. Maybe leave California for a minute."

Paul turned to him, nodding. "Yeah. I understand."

"If you still need me around, I won't go anywhere," Peter said.

"You're always welcome here, Kid. But don't feel like you have to hang around if you'd rather go somewhere else."

"Do you remember Simon? He wants to get out of California. We'll drive through Wyoming first, and then figure it out. I know it's quick, but we were thinking of leaving later today." Peter hadn't thought about how Paul might react, but he watched Paul thinking. He and Paul had spent a lot of time not talking about Simon and Peter's blind spot for him.

Paul reached into his jacket pocket, pulling out an envelope and handing it to Peter. "This seems like a decent time to hand this over." Peter opened the envelope to find a cashier's check for $5000.

"What's this?" Peter asked, looking at the check.

"Apparently your mom had me as a beneficiary for some old 401k she'd forgotten to roll over, and I got a check in the mail a few days ago," Paul said, "I might not have been able to help with the bills that came in, but you deserve this more than I do."

Even after the insurance money, this was the most money that Peter had seen in a long time without having to think about using it to pay off medical bills.

"Are you sure, Paul?"

"With how much you took care of your mom through everything, it's not enough. It's a start though, and I thought you'd want to use it to head back to Sacramento or look into a trade school like you talk about sometimes; leaving California might be a good option though, if that's what you want."

"Thanks." Peter slid the cashier's check into his pocket.

"So, about Simon," Paul hesitated for a moment, "I've got to ask. Are you sure about him?"

"I don't know. He's been having a hard time, and just needs someone to help get him out of here. I'm the best option he's got."

"He could do a lot worse," Paul said with a smile, "Just remember that he's not the best option you've got, ok? Not necessarily."

"Thanks Paul."

"You'll always have a place here if you need it, but sometimes we all need a fresh start." Paul gave Peter a solid pat on the shoulder, before heading to the Living Room.

The next few hours passed quickly as Peter worked to get everything in order. With a fair amount of the day left, Peter decided to explore the used bookstore in town for anything he could find on Wyoming. It wasn't a surprise to find the selection pretty slim, but he did manage to find an old road map and a worn old book of short stories about the Rocky Mountain States. He also found a gardening book with a faded cover. Whether they actually made it to where they were heading, any random spot they ended up at seemed likely to have enough dirt to try growing something.

When Peter pulled into the restaurant parking lot, it was five minutes to seven. The old truck was gassed up, double checked, and everything Peter thought they'd need was stowed securely and tied down in the truck bed. He made sure to leave enough room in the back for anything that Simon might choose to bring along. While the odds were decent that Simon's things would only consist of a toothbrush and two changes of underwear, Peter thought it best to be prepared for the possibility that Simon decided to pack an actual bag or two. With the summer sun shining through his window, Peter gazed over the road map to plot the most and least efficient routes through the state.

When the clock on his radio read ten after seven, Peter's phone rang.

"Hey." Simon's voice sounded small on the other end of the phone.

"Hey, are you hiding back there somewhere? I thought you got off at seven."

There was silence for a moment, and in the background Peter could hear the familiar sound of a hospital speaker shouting something he couldn't make out.

"I got a call from the hospital about an hour into my shift. I'm the only person listed on my dad's emergency contact sheet." Peter didn't need to hear anything else before he turned the truck's ignition and pulled out of the parking lot.

By law, you need to be at least one hundred feet away from the entrance of a hospital to smoke; if he were to measure, Peter would bet that Simon stood exactly one hundred and one feet away from the hospital door. When Simon saw Peter, he barely turned to acknowledge Peter walking over.

"What happened?"

"It was a heart attack. One of the neighbors called an ambulance, and a nurse called me." Simon's face made it clear that his dad wouldn't be shrugging this off like past scares.

"How is he?"

"He needed emergency surgery, but they say he'll be fine now."

"That's good." Peter tried to put his arm around Simon, but he shook it off.

"It's not going to happen, Peter. We can't leave tonight."

"That's alright. We'll leave after he gets better."

"He won't get better for a while," Simon said.

"I don't care. Waiting doesn't change anything for me."

"It changes things for me, Peter. It makes things different. It was a nice couple of days, but that's all done now."

"You can't really believe that."

"What's it matter what I believe?" Simon paused, taking a last drag of his cigarette before dropping it to the ground. "I've got to get back in there, and you should probably go. A few people from church are coming over to pray. They'll be here any minute." Simon stomped out his cigarette and walked inside the hospital without looking back.

Climbing inside his truck, Peter rolled down one of the windows. He looked at the roadmap and the two books that sat on the passenger seat. The dense summer heat began to creep into the truck. Pulling out of the hospital parking lot, Peter drove past Paul's house on his way to the freeway. The cab felt a little big for one person as Peter merged onto the highway, but maybe it wouldn't feel that way by the time he reached Wyoming or perhaps even Illinois.

THE LESSER

IT WAS RAINING WHEN HE AND KELLY HAD GONE TO SLEEP, and Evan couldn't tell if the rain in the morning was the same barrage of water or if it was something new. The sudden storm had been unexpectedly fierce, providing much-needed water at the worst possible time. He hadn't expected to check on his parents' house while they were away, until the third straight day of heavy rain. The windows of Kelly's apartment reminded him of a drive-thru car wash every time he turned to look outside, and a splash of suds would not have been too surprising. Evan half-rolled over, as Kelly rose out of bed.

"Your phone's blinking." Kelly said, her footsteps softly making their way to the bathroom. Evan grabbed his phone from the top of the nightstand while Kelly brushed her teeth.

Since you don't work today, check on the house? Heard there's a lot of rain. It was simple and direct. In everything his parents did, there was a calmness that rarely betrayed anything below the surface. Evan looked through all of the messages his parents had sent in the last several weeks, a catalog of reminders and expectations. All parts of the larger plan, and everything fitting together.

There's a lot to be done before the Fall. Your father and I have already started talking about it.

You'll get in somewhere with enough applications.

Have you heard from any more schools yet?

I talked to a friend at the firm. He'll write a reference for you.

You'll need a reference from a professor. Which class gave you the best grade?

Your personal statement doesn't stand out enough. I'll add some things in.

Michigan State has an open-house event, so take the weekend of the 24th off work.

Your list of schools is too ambitious. I'm going to add in some safe options.

Evan didn't respond to his mother's latest message, instead placing the phone back on the nightstand. Unwilling to accept that storms or accidents can't be planned for, they always seemed surprised at the idea that some things didn't work out like they expected.

"Did we have specific plans today?" Evan asked.

Kelly spat a mouthful of toothpaste into the sink. "There was going to be a farmer's market, but I'm guessing that's pretty well cancelled."

"How would you feel about swinging by my parents' house and making sure it hasn't floated away yet?" Evan rose out of the bed, scanning the floor until he found his pants.

"Would they be ok with me being there?" Kelly placed her toothbrush back in the toothbrush holder, running a hand over her hair to flatten down some of the uneven parts.

"Sure," Evan pulled his pants up, "why wouldn't they?"

"We can keep not talking about it if you want," she shrugged, "but we should at least admit that they don't like me. We don't have to get into it, but let's at least be upfront. Ok?" In the five months that he and Kelly had been together, Evan's parents had continued putting off meeting her. The excuses had started out as reasonable enough in the beginning, ranging from headaches to long days at work to car trouble. They'd lost the subtlety in recent weeks, becoming vocal that their interest lie in Evan's law school rejections rather than some college girlfriend he would surely lose track of in the coming fall.

"It's not that they don't like you—" Evan started, and then stopped himself. Standing in front of her closet, Kelly turned back toward him as she stepped into a pair of jeans and pulled them up to her waist. Wearing the same loose shirt she'd slept in, her half-sleeve tattoo spat color across her right arm just below where the shirt fabric ended. "They just like their plans and have a hard time factoring anyone into them."

"Like I said, we don't have to talk about it just yet," walking back over to the bed, she leaned across it and gave him a kiss on the cheek, "but we'll probably have to at some point." Evan had already been through the big meeting with Kelly's family months ago, visiting at least a dozen times since. With his dad's work conference this week, it would at least put the conversation off a little longer. One of several conversations.

"Yeah, we will."

"Good, and that reminds me. My mom wants you over for dinner again soon, she thinks you're too skinny." Kelly grabbed a hoodie from her closet.

"Am I too skinny?" Evan looked down at his shirtless stomach.

"A few pounds here or there couldn't hurt." Kelly grinned, as she picked his shirt up from the floor and threw it to him. "She says you look like you've never had a home-cooked meal in your life, whatever that's supposed to mean."

HIS PARENT'S CUL-DE-SAC WAS A DESERT OF CONCRETE, wood chips, and old irrigation that made it hard for the drains to keep up with the steady downpour of water. As Evan stepped out of Kelly's car, puddles pooled together on the sidewalk. Bypassing the house itself, Evan's first stop was the small keypad on the outside of his parents' garage. After he typed in the code, the garage door groaned slightly as it lifted up. Evan passed through the garage, heading into the small backyard to look at the old shed that had come with the house. When Evan opened the doors of the small shed, the cardboard boxes and plywood floor all looked too damp to ignore. Even as the rain began to slow down, there was a steady drip of water from the roof of the shed onto the boxes.

"What's the verdict?" Kelly asked, joining Evan in the backyard.

"My parents probably can't put off replacing this shed any longer, but I'm more concerned about the boxes right now; if it warms up and they just sit until my parents get back, they'll be covered in mold by the time my parents get around to them. I should run up to the store and get some new boxes," He wasn't even sure what was in the boxes, but the contents wouldn't likely survive another two days of waiting for his parents to return, "But these boxes should get moved into the garage before worrying about new boxes."

"I can help out for a bit, if you want?" Kelly asked.

"Are you sure you don't mind?"

"You're lucky I don't have to work today," Kelly grinned, her short brown hair shining with rain. Bending down to wrap her arms around a cardboard box, Kelly nudged the door gently with her shoulder as she went back into the garage. "Besides, I like rifling through other people's random junk."

"Well, it looks like we've got plenty of that in here."

"I'm expecting a movie in exchange for manual labor though," Kelly shouted back at him through the open door that led into the garage. Evan grabbed a box as the rain lightly tapped against the shed.

Once the shed was empty, the dozen cubes of soggy cardboard sat in lines across the garage floor. He and Kelly worked through each of the boxes separately, moving the random assortments of keepsakes or holiday decorations onto the concrete floor. As Evan debated whether or not to untangle a string of Christmas lights to place neatly in a new box later, Kelly began to laugh with excitement as she moved to the latest box in front of her. From a few feet away, he could see *Evan* written on the side of the box in faded marker.

"And here's what I was looking for all along. Five months in, but I've finally found some dirt," she said with a tone of triumph as he walked over. "Maybe this will make us even for that time my mom pulled out the home movies. I can't wait to see what kind of bowl cut you had or which horrible fashion choices your parents inflicted upon you." Before he could say anything, she had already flipped the soggy flaps of the box open to find a school photo of a small sixth grader. The boy and Evan had some of the same features, but the boy's eyes were a bright blue to Evan's brown. She looked up at him, confusion across her face.

"Who's this?" She asked, her voice quieter than its normal joyful volume.

"That's my brother." Evan walked to her, standing over the box as Kelly rose to her feet. "Evan."

"You have a brother also named Evan?"

"I never met him," he said, bending down to open the box again. There was a random assortment of elementary school track ribbons that Evan had never won and tests that Evan had never taken. "He died before I was born."

"I'm—" Kelly placed her hand on his shoulder. "Why would they name you that?"

"We never talk about it." Evan began to remove the random keepsakes from the box, as Kelly stood over him. "It's ok. We'll need to take these out anyway."

"I'm sorry, Evan. I just saw your name on the side, and..." She looked down at the box, as Evan rose to his feet.

"Kelly?"

She looked up to meet his eyes.

"It's really ok." Evan leaned over to kiss her on the cheek.

Evan couldn't remember how old he was before he stopped assuming that other families included an older brother the way his did. Evan's brother had shaped the basic outline of his life; as most older siblings seemed to do, Evan's brother set all the precedents that shaped the plans his parents would build for the future. Even when a car accident threatened to destroy those plans, Evan's parents found a way to keep their plans intact. Through all of the ill-fitting clothes and out-of-style toys, those plans always felt larger than any one child. His parents had accepted their reality and seemed to assume that Evan would as well, even when that reality included naming a child after his brother who would stay twelve forever.

Evan and Kelly removed the contents of the box in silence, placing the random collection of old photos and memorabilia on the concrete floor of the garage. He kept the school photo on top of the assorted memories, with the boy smiling big in a way that Evan rarely did. Evan tried to get a conversation going again after the box, but it felt too forced. They worked in silence until the garage had an arrangement of random items spread across a dozen piles. Against one of the walls, the soggy cardboard was stacked high.

"I'm sorry about earlier," Kelly said, as Evan picked himself up from the garage floor. "Can I ask something that you might not want to answer?" Kelly had always done this; it's harder to avoid uncomfortable questions after agreeing to walk directly into them.

"Yeah."

"Why didn't you tell me about this before?"

Evan shrugged. "Kind of hard to know how to bring it up with people." In the past, similar conversations had not gone well. Evan had learned that some family secrets don't do well in the light.

"I'm not people though," Kelly placed her hand on his shoulder, "I'm Kelly."

"Yeah," he said softly, placing his hand over hers.

"That's pretty fucked up. It's ok to say that, right?"

"Yeah." Evan's parents had never really talked about why they held to a single name across two children. It may have felt like a spell being cast or a ritual being performed, gathering together all of the right ingredients and going through the right motions in order to turn back time. Once he was old enough to recognize what was happening, Evan felt powerless to go against the tide of memories pushing him toward someone else's life. Evan's brother had laid down a path that seemed natural for his parents to fall back into. On those rare occasions that Evan had mustered the energy to push back against these plans, his parents reacted with a redoubled commitment to the life they had decided on for him; it was the kind of resolve that can make you doubt yourself.

"It's alright," She placed her hand on his elbow as she stood up, leaving it there, "You just rarely talk about your family or how you're feeling, which isn't how my family operates at all. Hell, my sister still won't shut up about some doll I put in the garbage disposal when we were little."

"My parents don't talk about things," Evan gestured in Kelly's direction, "They never talk about what happened with him, either. It doesn't take long before a kid learns which things he's not supposed to question."

"We can talk about that stuff though, if that's what you want."

"Thanks."

"Or we can not talk about it too," Kelly smiled, "either way though, I'm definitely adding food to my demands of compensation for all this work."

Evan laughed, as they closed the garage door behind them and headed to Kelly's car.

It wasn't until they had returned with a dozen new boxes that they had any reason to walk through the main house. They managed to grab lunch and pick up new boxes during a brief break in the rain and worked to keep the new cardboard mostly dry by running from Kelly's car to the house. Kelly spotted the open envelope first, passing through the kitchen with both arms hugging a pile of cardboard.

"Hey, it looks like your parents left some mail out," she said, dropping the new boxes onto the carpet in the living room.

Evan spotted the envelope right away as he walked close, addressed to him and already opened. The envelope had been neatly left on the counter, the seal of the University of Wisconsin's law school glossy in the corner of the envelope. His father's handwriting was scrawled across the top of the envelope: *Congratulations.*

He walked past the kitchen to set his boxes on top of the pile Kelly had already started, before turning back to pick up the envelope.

"Seems a bit odd that they'd send the letter here," Kelly said.

"I listed my parents' place as my permanent address, so maybe they thought it was a safer bet than my apartment." Evan shrugged, pulling the letter out of its envelope to read quickly. The form letter had his name typed at the top, highlighting how selective the program was and the fact that many others had been turned down so that the school could offer him admittance for the upcoming Fall semester.

"Hooray?" She asked, as she stepped into the kitchen behind him.

"Yeah," Evan placed the letter back down on the counter, "thanks."

"So that's all of the law schools then?"

"Yeah." Seventeen law schools. His December had been overwhelmed with gathering all of the required documents for seventeen different law school applications, but Wisconsin was the only acceptance. Even though there had been sixteen rejections, it had eased the burden to know that there were sixteen schools he no longer needed to worry about.

"Any news on that other program?"

"I got an email last week that they're wrapping things up, so I'll probably hear something soon." Evan's dad had led the charge on working through the law school applications, helping to rework the personal statements without much input from Evan. His parents had been convinced that Pre-Law would set Evan up for success, but it was easy to imagine those seventeen law schools facing an unending wave of Pre-Law applicants every year. There was only one program he had applied to that wasn't a law school – the only application that his parents hadn't paid for. In all his research into law Schools, he had also found Purdue University's Philosophy Department. He applied to the master's program randomly, without much expectation other than finally having an application where his Pre-Law major would stand out.

"My roommate didn't hear back on her grad applications until the end of March last year, so there's still time," Kelly said hopefully.

"Did you think I was crazy when I told you about applying for a master's program in Philosophy?" Early on into their dating, she had grown used to the sight of him stressing over application materials, but hadn't raised an eyebrow when he mentioned Purdue's program.

"Sometimes, we need to let the crazy burn itself out." She smiled, placing a hand on his shoulder.

"Thanks," Evan said.

"Keep supporting my lack of ambition, and I can support just about anything." Having bounced from one major to the next throughout her time in school, finally settling on a General Studies degree had taken the pressure off Kelly. She'd graduate a year later than Evan, but the random hodgepodge of courses collected on her transcript seemed to suit her. Unlike everything Evan had been taught, the plans Kelly made seemed to buckle under the weight of who she was. "Besides, it doesn't matter; not if this is something you want to do."

"Would you rather come visit me in Wisconsin or Indiana?"

"As long as there's a good farmer's market nearby, we'll figure out the rest." She patted his shoulder gently, before stepping away from the kitchen toward the pile of new boxes.

"Do you remember that paper I had to write last fall, the one for my Comparative Religion class?" They each took a spot on the carpet and started putting the new boxes together.

"I remember you telling me a bit about it," she said as she tossed a completed box to her right, "that's the one you submitted for the Philosophy program, right?"

"Yeah. I was looking at all of the apostles and how they fit into the bigger picture of the New Testament, and I guess I never realized that there were two apostles named James."

"Yeah," Kelly reached for a new box to put together, "we had to learn them all in Sunday school, so I can still recite them in order." She grimaced slightly at the thought.

"I really started to focus in on James the Lesser, and how little there was about him. The other James played a much bigger part, but there was just something about the fact that the best anyone could do for that apostle was to emphasize who he wasn't. Everything about this one man, wrapped up in how he fell short of the other."

"Yeah, that makes sense." Kelly looked up from the box she was putting together.

"I never thought any Philosophy program would pay much attention to a Pre-Law degree, and maybe they won't." Evan finished his box and reached for a new one.

"Or maybe they will."

It was dark by the time they finished moving the piles of things into the new boxes, with twelve cardboard islands floating neatly in the living room's sea of carpet. They drove to his apartment, Kelly's car pulling in behind his own he had left there.

Later that night, Kelly was the first one to fall asleep and Evan listened to the sound of the rain against the windows. When Evan was in High School, he developed a habit of taking long walks around the neighborhood. Those long walks turned into long drives on those nights when he couldn't sleep. Evan got out of bed slowly, careful to not be louder than the rain outside. Leaving a quick note on the nightstand, he got dressed and left the apartment. Evan pulled his phone from his pocket and placed it in his car's cup holder, ignoring the phone's blinking light as he drove out of the apartment complex parking lot.

He hadn't planned on driving anywhere specific, but it felt natural to go back to his parents' house. Evan flipped on one light after the other, until every room he walked through shone brightly out into the night. From the boxes in the living room, he only grabbed one and separated it from the others. Walking away from the kitchen and down the hall, he stopped at the spare room that used to be his bedroom. Evan set the box down at his feet, opening the closet to reveal a collection of boxes all with his brother's name written across the side.

Standing apart from the boxes on the shelf was an old photo album, and Evan pulled it down. Among all the pictures he had seen hundreds of times before, the one that stood out the most was Evan's brother and his father standing side-by-side. They wore matching brown suits, with a miniature suitcase to ensure that father and son were a perfect matching set. Evan's brother and his father both smiled wide for the camera, with a happiness that Evan couldn't remember seeing in his father. He flipped the picture over to find *Career Day: October 10, 1993,*written across the back.

At the back of the album was just one picture of his brother's grave. *Evan Jones 1982-1994: Beloved son, never to be forgotten.*

Evan couldn't remember ever seeing the grave in person, and it would have been long ago if it ever happened at all. Evan had been born in a new town, in a new house far away from the car accident that had spared both his parents. They worked to create distance from everything they had known before, except for that name written on a gravestone a few towns over. There was so much Evan couldn't ask his parents, so much that they had never been willing to talk about. Evan closed the album, placing it back on the shelf.

Opening the box on the floor, Evan reached into his pocket to pull out the acceptance letter from Wisconsin, reading it again. There was nothing about him in the letter, nothing on why he'd been chosen over all of the other applicants. The letter offered a firm acceptance deadline next week, with insistence that no exceptions would be made if this deadline passed. He placed the letter on top of everything else in the box, the university seal covering his brother's face as Evan closed the cardboard flaps. There were now seventeen schools he no longer needed to worry about. Moving to a junk drawer in the room, Evan removed a marker and neatly wrote *Evan's Stuff* on the side. There was just enough room to fit the box alongside the others, while still closing the closet door.

Evan turned off the lights in the house, before locking the front door. The rain had started to lessen, but his shoulders caught small drops of water as he walked back to his car. Settling behind the steering wheel, Evan saw his phone still blinking a reminder.

We need to find you an internship this summer. Maybe at my firm.

Evan reached for the volume knob on the dash, turning the music up slightly as he placed his phone back in the cupholder. He thought of the picture of his dad and brother, and his dad's smile. Both parents long ago tempered any broad swings of emotion, never acknowledging how they felt. Even when they got mad, they wouldn't admit to being mad. Even when they were disappointed, they'd never put words to those feelings. The emotions instead hung in the air, a problem for Evan to solve by better adhering to the plan.

As soon as they got back, his parents would notice the acceptance letter gone from the counter. If the acceptance deadline came and went, he wouldn't start at Wisconsin in the Fall. How would they react, knowing that Evan finally shook up their plans beyond repair? He wanted them to say they were mad, to tell him they were disappointed. At least then, they'd all be able to agree that Evan was different from the brother he'd never met.

WINDFALL

It would be hard to not notice the old Brown Pontiac idling across the street, a stark contrast from the newer minivans and SUVs in the neighborhood. It catches my eye as soon as I turn the corner for my house, the spots of rust on the back of the car standing out against the late winter snow on the ground. It has an Illinois plate, a sharp yellow contrast to the Indiana plate on my own car. The driver's arm hangs out of the open window, and he pulls it in to take a drag from his cigarette right as my garage door closes.

As I step out of my car, I can hear Jeremy laughing from the kitchen. Walking into the house, I see Jeremy and my dad at the kitchen table; piles of pretzel sticks are spread out before them, with a deck of cards in front of my dad. The table is uncharacteristically empty of random crayons or school supplies, all of those stowed away to make a suitable Blackjack table. My dad never seems more himself than when he has his hands on a deck of cards, and he has a confidence on his face I remember from all those times I sat next to him at a card table. For as long as I can remember, my dad's luck was something beyond question. He always saw it as lasting not as long as it should, and I only realized as I got older that he would always ignore a good run in the hopes of an even better one.

"Dad!" Jeremy yells, as I open the door. "Happy birthday, Dad." All fifty pounds of him crash into my leg, as he wraps it in a hug. I had to leave for work before he was up this morning, and he looks like he's been waiting all day to give me his birthday wishes.

"Thanks, buddy. What are you up to?"

"Grandpa's teaching me cards. He says luck runs in our family." Jeremy only ever sees this side of my dad: the showman and the card shark, who'll dazzle everyone with stories and flare before finding the nearest casino in search of that big payout. These visits were a lot less common for a long time, until my dad landed nearby last year after his girlfriend burned all of his stuff in West Virginia and his car broke down on his way to Nebraska. I sent him enough money for a bus ticket and the kind of stay-by-the-week hotel that he always liked more than our couch; Melissa and I agreed a long time ago that he gets $300 a year, no matter how many emergencies come up. His lack of a car hasn't kept him away from the nearest casino.

"Yeah, he always did say that," I say, walking toward the kitchen, "it sometimes skips a generation or two though, right Dad?"

"Happy birthday, Bobby," my dad greets me with the same ear-to-ear smile that always made it easy for him to make friends at a table, raking a few pretzels toward him. "How's my favorite upstanding citizen?"

"Doing as well as ever," I say, loosening my tie. Last March, I realized that I'd been a security guard longer than my dad had ever held any single job. When I became a supervisor last year, my dad couldn't bring himself to say he was proud. I think he wanted to, but I could see the confusion on his face as he tried to figure out why anyone would want to go from being a gate guard to being in charge of security at the warehouse. He never saw work as anything more than a way to pay for that next round of Blackjack. "You're early, Dad. I hope you don't mind waiting while we get ready."

"I'm never early or late, Bobby. I'm only ever exactly on time. Didn't I teach you better than that?"

"Yeah, Dad." On the table in front of them, I can see Jeremy's pile of pretzels is pretty small compared to my dad's pile. If I had to guess, I would say this hasn't gone on for more than a few hands. "Isn't six a bit young for Blackjack?" I ask.

"I'll be seven soon, Dad," Jeremy says, as my dad deals a new hand.

"The boy has a point. Besides, it's just for pretzels." This time it's for pretzels.

"I'm glad you two are having so much fun. Where's mom, buddy?" I ask, looking around the kitchen.

"I'm up here, Robert." Melissa says, walking down the stairs. "Did you have a good day at work?"

"I did. How was your day?"

"A few things here and there." she says, giving me a light kiss on the cheek.

"Have you guys been having fun with my dad for long?"

"Only for about ten minutes. It was such a pleasant surprise to see Bob waiting for us when Jeremy and I got home. He offered to watch Jeremy while I wrapped up some things, but I thought you were going to play *Go Fish*, Bob?"

"That may have been the initial thought," my dad grins, "but the boy here should know a few things about a real card game."

"Wasn't the plan also to meet at the restaurant, Dad?" I ask, watching him deal out the hand.

"Never been one for plans. You know how I like to keep things exciting, Bobby." My dad laughs, before turning his attention back to Jeremy. He has a nine turned face up, his other card hidden. "Now remember, you can see I have a nine, but you can't see what else I have. When do you ask for a new card?"

Jeremy thinks for a moment, counting on his fingers. "Now?" His cards lay out on the table, showing an eight and a six.

My dad laughs. "That's right." He draws a card, flipping it up to reveal a three that he lays on top of Jeremy's six. "Well, that's alright for now. You've got a good hand here with a total of seventeen. Do you think that can beat what I've got?"

Jeremy studies the cards carefully, before turning to me. "Dad?"

"It's risky, buddy. Grandpa might say there are a few cards that will help you win, but sometimes we need to trust what we know without hoping for luck." After I was old enough to take care of myself, it became harder and harder to believe in my dad or his luck. His luck was something that he saw in the deepest part of himself, just as much a part of him as the beer gut bumping against the card table.

"But you have to wonder if your luck will come through for you." My dad offers, grinning at Jeremy. "If we don't risk it, we won't win."

"Hit me!" Jeremy shouts with excitement, as my dad flips over a six.

"And busted. Your dad never trusted luck, but he's always been the sensible one in the family, haven't you Bobby?" My dad flips over his card to reveal a seven with one hand as he scoops some of Jeremy's pretzels with the other. "But at least it's just pretzels. Boy, could I tell you some stories." He says with a chuckle.

"Maybe save some of those stories for a few years down the road, Bob?" Melissa offers.

"Oh, definitely," he laughs, "this has been a lot of fun though; so much fun that I forgot to ask you how things have been at the library."

"Things are good, Bob." Melissa works at a literacy non-profit, and has since before Jeremy was born. She's never worked at a library, but long ago gave up trying to correct him. "Thanks for asking. How are things with you?"

"You know me," he says simply, starting to deal out another hand. "Want to win some of your pretzels back, Kiddo?" Jeremy's eyes get big with excitement, but Melissa walks over and places a hand on my dad's shoulder.

"I think there's probably been enough cards for now, Bob," Melissa says, "we should head out to the restaurant to meet my parents."

Jeremy starts to protest, but my dad scoops up the cards and shuffles them neatly back into a deck. "No, Kiddo, your mom's right. One thing I've learned is that there are always more card games, but you should never pass up a good meal."

"Are you excited for your birthday dinner, Dad?" Jeremy asks, grabbing a pretzel when he thinks no one is looking.

"Yeah, it'll be fun for all of us to get together."

"Actually, that's part of why I came over." As soon as my dad speaks, I see a look of recognition on Melissa's face. It reminds me of when he missed our rehearsal dinner because the table was too hot to ignore, and why he never even made it to Jeremy's first birthday at all. She and I both know what's coming, but Jeremy's still a few years away from piecing it all together.

"Come on, Sweetie," Melissa says to Jeremy, "we need to get you ready."

"Ok," Jeremy jumps up from his chair, "can I sit next to Grandpa at dinner?"

"We'll figure out where everyone sits when we get to the restaurant." Melissa places her hand on Jeremy's shoulder, guiding him up the stairs. "Great to see you, Bob."

"Always a pleasure." My dad and I both watch them disappear up the stairs, as my dad's phone buzzes in his pocket. He pulls out his phone and sends a quick text, before putting the phone away again. "You've got a good one there, Bobby. Trust me on this; I've had more than my fair share of bad ones." He smiles for a second, but I watch as the smile starts to fade.

"So what's up, dad?"

"I can't actually stay that long, but I wanted to give you this." He pulls out two unsealed envelopes, handing them both to me. I can feel stiff cardboard inside both envelopes. One is for me and I notice that the other envelope is for Jeremy, even though his birthday isn't for another month. "And for the kiddo too."

"Thanks," I place the envelopes on the counter, "but it's a bit early for him, isn't it?"

"Well, that's the thing. I'll probably be back by then, but just in case I'm not, I wanted the kid to have something." He looks down for a moment. "There's a lucky break out in Wyoming, at one of those Indian casinos. Turns out that there was this big flash flood that took out half of a town near the casino, so they need warm bodies to keep the place staffed. Manning the roulette wheel is landing people $30 an hour, just so the place doesn't have to close down for a couple weeks. My friend Meth Head Chuck and I have to get out there soon."

"Meth Head Chuck?"

"Don't worry, it's just a name. You don't want to confuse him with Pills Chuck; it's a touchy issue," He laughs. "We met down at that bar near my hotel."

"That's Chuck idling across the street?" Walking to the window near the front door, I look out at the old brown Pontiac still waiting on the other side of the street. The man behind the wheel must have lit up a new cigarette since I pulled into the garage. I'm sure the neighbor across the street will find a small pile of cigarette butts on the ground the next time he goes to check the mail. From this angle, I can see that Chuck's unkempt hair almost reaches his shoulders.

"Yeah, we need to get there before all the other vultures swoop in." My dad watches me examine his friend, walking over to playfully pat my shoulder. "He's a good guy; you'd like him."

"You've got a place lined up?"

"Yeah," he says, shifting on his feet. "Well, no…not really. We've got a plan though, and we'll rake in the money if we sleep in his car for a bit. Chuck's got blankets ready to go and everything. Wyoming isn't as bad as it could be this time of year."

"Jeremy was really looking forward to seeing you."

"Yeah, you've got yourself a good kid there. A good wife too. No one needs me hanging around." He looks down at his feet again, and I almost wonder if he is trying to think his way out of chasing his next round of good fortune. "Anyway…This is the lucky break I've needed for a while."

When I was young, my dad's luck was a matter of faith: something to be taken as fact despite all other evidence. He saw it as clearly as prophecy, envisioning those moments in which his luck would pay off after all the times that would have shaken anyone less devoted. In all the ways that a boy can believe his father, I wanted to go a step further: I wanted to believe in him as he saw himself, with the same conviction that his time would come. At Four years old, I wanted to believe that it was normal for adults to not eat dinner as long as there was enough spare change around for a Happy Meal. At Seven years old, I was as certain as I could be that the only real losers are the ones who never even play. At Nine, it made sense that Christmas had to be a bit light sometimes, because it would all be worth it once he took his next check to the Blackjack table. At Eleven, I started to see that there would never be enough luck for all his ambitions. No good run would ever last long enough, and he'd be back to scrounging up enough to barely get by.

"And if this lucky break doesn't pan out?"

"Well, nothing's a guarantee these days." We can hear Melissa and Jeremy rustling upstairs. "I'll find a way to land on my feet though. I always have, haven't I?"

"Yeah, Dad."

"Besides," he slaps my shoulder playfully, "My favorite upstanding citizen is only a collect call away, if things get dicey. It'll be fine though, I can feel it. Then I'll come back here and make it up to you." He could be thinking of any number of things to make up to me, beyond tonight. It doesn't matter though, I stopped keeping track a long time ago.

"You don't have to make it up to me, Dad."

"I do, Bobby. You know I've always tried my best, don't you Bobby?" He's looking at the door now, his gaze focused on the knob. "You're a better man by far, but I've always tried my best."

"I know."

"Anyways," he shakes his head, as though to clear it, "I feel that good luck now. It's gonna get me back to where I need to be, and then I'll be here for the kiddo's birthday. Or Christmas. We'll figure it out." I watch as he hesitates for a final moment, not moving toward the door. Maybe he wants me to try and talk him out of it, to convince Chuck to drive on alone. If he didn't leave tonight, some other lucky break would come calling before long. There were years I hoped he'd finally get that windfall so he could stop chasing it and years I'd wanted him to be more like the dads I saw on TV, but none of that matters anymore. For all the gambled paychecks and broken promises, he's still the parent who stayed.

"Good luck, Dad," I say, extending my hand.

"You're a good man, Bobby. Better than I ever deserved." He gives my hand a hearty shake, and slaps my shoulder with his other hand. "I should get going though. I told Chuck this little detour would only slow us down twenty minutes." He chuckles as he opens the door and walks across the street. I watch the Pontiac drive away, metal music screaming from its old speakers as they disappear around a corner.

After I close the door, I walk back to the kitchen and look at the envelopes. Pulling Jeremy's card from its envelope, there is a cartoon

Dinosaur that seems too excited even for a kid's birthday. The card has a big number seven on the front, and a brief message inside: *Happy birthday, Scout. Enjoy the money, and don't spend it all in one place. Grandpa.* There isn't any money inside the card, and nothing in the envelope either. I grab a twenty from my wallet, placing it inside the card; maybe my dad would say he forgot to put the money in or maybe he'd say that he'll put it in when he gets back from Wyoming, but this has happened enough times that we both know I won't risk Jeremy opening up an empty card. I seal up the envelope and put it in a kitchen drawer.

The card my dad left for me is larger, with a scratcher on the inside. I see his loose handwriting inside, scribbled quickly: *Bobby, I got this just for you. I had my friend drive me around to six different gas stations before I found the one that felt right. Ya know how it just feels like a winner? Here's that big winner, for my big winner. I feel it in my bones, but do me a favor ok? Don't scratch it off until I'm back from Wyoming. I want to be there when you see your old man's luck pay off.* I look at the scratcher, which promises a grand prize of half a million dollars, and stuff it into my pocket.

Upstairs, I can hear Jeremy protesting, "But I don't want to wear a jacket. It's not even that cold out."

For a few years I don't remember, my dad said he had something close to a career back before my mom left. Any memories of either my mom or his career have long been washed away, gone by the time I was old enough to understand that not everyone spent all of their free time at racetracks and blackjack tables. He always said that people like him were meant for more, and that a day job was just there to make sure he would have the money for when his luck finally came through; it's hard to forget how much disdain he always had for mortgages and 401Ks and all the things Melissa and I have worked for. No matter how much he made or how many times a windfall came through, I knew that he would never be content with walking away from a hot table. He could manage to hold back only enough to keep a roof over our heads, but never enough to walk away completely.

"Where's Grandpa?" Jeremy asks, seeing me alone in the kitchen when he comes down the stairs.

"He couldn't stay after all, Buddy. He did want to say that he's looking forward to the next time he can see you though."

"Put your shoes on so we can go," Melissa tells Jeremy, as she walks down the stairs behind him carrying his overnight bag, "and you haven't told your dad the big news yet."

"Yeah?" I ask.

"I'm staying the night with Nana and Papa. We packed a bag, so I can go with them after the restaurant," Jeremy says.

"That'll be a lot of fun, buddy."

"Are you doing ok?" Melissa asks quietly, after walking over. "It's alright to be mad at him."

"I'm not mad though, it's just my dad being my dad."

"Well, he chose some good timing."

"He always does." I shrug.

"Yeah." She squeezes my shoulder softly. She doesn't need to say anything else because we've had that conversation before.

"What are you two whispering about?" Jeremy asks, walking over in his boots.

"Well," I say, crouching down to be eye level with him, "I was just telling mom that I'm going to eat all of the cake at the restaurant, and I don't think I'll share any of it. That's ok, right?"

"No!" He protests. "I want the cake too."

"Enough worrying about cake," Melissa says, kissing me on the cheek. "Nana and Papa will be there waiting for us if we take too long."

"I'm not going if there isn't cake," Jeremy says, pretending to be firm in his outrage.

"No?" I ask.

"No." His grin is big and careless.

"Well, that's it then," I stand back up, "I guess we can't go to the restaurant if Jeremy isn't coming too."

"Is that so?" Melissa asks, slipping on her shoes at the door.

"Well…" Jeremy offers helpfully, "I'll go if there's cake."

I place my hand on my chin, carefully considering what to do. "Actually, there is another thing we haven't thought of yet."

"What?" Jeremy asks.

"This!" I say, picking him up and draping him over one shoulder. "I guess we'll just have to fly you into the car."

"Put me down. Put me down." He yells happily as I spin in place. Once I set him down, he looks back up at me. "Ok, one more time."

"Ok then." I pick him back up and spin around quickly until his size thirteen snow boots start kicking in the air.

"Are you two almost done?" Melissa asks, with a smile.

"I guess it's time to eat, buddy." I set Jeremy back down on the floor. "Are you getting hungry?"

"I'm sooo hungry. I want to order a whole chicken tonight at dinner."

"I'm hungry too, but we'll see about that chicken," I say, as I put my shoes on.

Melissa puts Jeremy in the car, and I lock the door behind me. I wonder how far my dad and Meth Head Chuck will make it by the time we finish dinner. If they avoid stopping much, they could be as far as Iowa by the time Melissa and I make it home later. I once drove fourteen hours from Texas to Indiana in a single energy drink-fueled night, but I have no idea how far away Wyoming is from Indiana. I've never been to Wyoming, and don't know much about the state other than the fact that it's about to get two more residents.

For as long as I can remember, chasing his luck has always been beyond question for my dad. The fact that I refused to chase that luck alongside him set things in motion for both of us. He always liked to say that some men wait for luck to happen to them, and others create it for themselves; I can agree with that, but I doubt my dad and I will ever be able to agree on which of us is creating his luck. As I climb into the passenger's seat, it's hard to not think about this new windfall my dad is chasing, all of the others that have come before, and the stiff cardboard of the scratcher in my pocket. Once we're at the restaurant, I'll drop the unscratched ticket on the ground. Maybe my dad's luck will pan out for someone else.

FORTY-FOUR WORDS:
OBITUARY DEPARTMENT VOICEMAILS
FROM JUNE 14TH -16TH

Message Received: June 14th, 5:26 pm

FRANKIE—HI, MY NAME IS FRANKIE and I just wanted to call about the obituary that ran in the paper for my brother David. I'm not totally sure why I'm even calling. Nothing in the paper was wrong, but I just feel like you missed so much. It's not like I expected you to gather all of the facts of his life into a block of print, but I guess I was hoping for more. The forty-four words in small black print seemed to say hardly anything about the brother we laid to rest earlier this afternoon.

Maybe it's unfair to have expected to see more of David in that obituary paragraph or more of what he left behind. It's weird. When David was born, I had been 4 at the time. I wasn't a fan at first, and I have this vivid memory of when I was 6; I wanted to put him in a cardboard box and ship him to wherever they kept the spare kids. My dad came home right as I was trying to figure out how many stamps would be appropriate for an 18-month-old and second-guessing my initial assumption that the post office would just know where to send the box if I got the number of stamps right. Even when I got old enough to know that you can't return a brother, we didn't always get along. Our personalities are—were very different. I like to be the center of attention and he did not. So it kind of worked out, when you think about it; growing up, I got a lot of the attention that he never even wanted in the first place.

It wasn't until I moved away to college that I started to appreciate him. A lot of people say that about their siblings, I guess. It's just how things tend to work out when you grow accustomed to someone always being there, it's hard to see who they're turning into until you take a step away. By the time I graduated from college, there was this serious man towering over me every time I came back to visit. Today was the first day I went back to my parents' house knowing that he wouldn't be there to greet me.

Message Received: June 14ᵗʰ, 7:53 pm

Tess —This is Tess from the Old West Bar, and I don't know who I talked to about the fire a few days after it happened. I'm not even sure if the people who asked about the fire said anything to the people who wrote the obituary. Maybe that's not how this sort of thing works, but shortly before his funeral I picked up a paper to read the obituary that you wrote for the man from last week's bar fire.

"David Lawry died in a fire on June 5ᵗʰ that began approximately around 9 pm at the Old West Bar in Harrison, California. The twenty-three-year-old Harrison resident is survived by his parents and sister. Though investigation is ongoing, no foul play is suspected."

I knew David for about two years from our time working at the bar; he liked to hide away in the kitchen, so most nights I could've been the only person he saw for any significant amount of time. Not too many people stuck around that place for as long as he and I did, so I got to know him pretty well.

David's actually the one who convinced me to go back to school, even after I'd given up on the idea. I enrolled at the same junior college he went to, and there were more than a few slow nights at work where he helped make sense of the homework I had to trudge through. For all of his help with my schoolwork, I introduced him to that drinking game King's Cup. I remember the first time I invited him over to my place on a rare night when neither of us had to work, and I get a call right as he's meant to show up. I figure that he'd got lost on the way to my apartment, but no – he was outside to let me know he was there, and just wanted to double-check that I was in 2c and not 2d. There's something quaint about a guy who would rather call you than risk knocking on the wrong door. We spent the night drinking while I told him all about this girlfriend who'd recently broken my heart, and he just let me keep talking until I'd gotten it all out. It was a good night.

David and I were friends, but it probably took some time working together before that happened. He's definitely the reason that I passed all of my English courses, since I could always count on him helping with the papers I had to write. He used to go through and clean things up so that I could say what I was trying to say, and the biggest mistake I always made was using the wrong tense. Draft after draft, I kept using the past tense to refer to what happened in these books or plays; draft after draft, he'd correct it. Eventually I was able to get him to explain that we need to think of what happens in a book or play as being in the present, because something is always in a state of happening. Hamlet is always going to be stabbing Polonius. Don Quixote is always going to be tilting at windmills.

He was a good friend in the ways I haven't had too many good friends, and I don't recognize him at all in that obituary.

Message Received: June 15ᵗʰ, 10:13 am
MR. JACOBS—I'M SORRY TO BE CALLING ON THE WEEKEND, but I just wanted to say something about the young man from yesterday's obituary. The man from the bar? I'm pretty sure he was a student of mine years ago, this short and quiet kid who liked to hide behind books too thick for the average 4ᵗʰ grader. After teaching for fifteen years, a lot of it can blend together. Some kids stick out in full detail, but usually only for the wrong reasons; for most of the others, it's just a random memory or two.

I woke up this morning to dig through fifteen years of school yearbooks until I found David's class from 2010. At that age, most of the kids smile big in a way that they'll hang onto until the awkwardness of junior high makes them embarrassed to be in the own skin. Not David though. He looked uncomfortable in front of the camera, without anyone or anything to take the attention away from him. It's random, but that's the sort of stuff that comes back to you when you recognize a face in the paper eleven years later.

When you teach 4ᵗʰ grade, you get used to the idea that kids become a big part of your life for a year and then they're gone. They don't tend to keep in touch, but occasionally you will get a student come back to visit a few years later. It tends to be the more outgoing kids, but I saw his picture next to the obituary in the paper and remembered this smart kid who did his best to stay out of the spotlight.

Message Received: June 15ᵗʰ, 1:29 pm
FRANKIE—MAYBE IT'S NOT FAIR TO EXPECT you to have written anything more than a brief summation of the events. Maybe I should have reached out sooner to let you know who you were writing about. For one thing, he would just let people talk and talk without feeling any kind of need to interject at all. Quiet is the word that comes to mind, but something like patience is probably closer to the reality. It was like he just took it all in, waiting for when that information would be useful. Maybe that's why he had such a great memory, honed from a childhood of listening while I announced every thought that came into my head.

Also, David stood by his decisions so much it would drive you crazy. He would take his time with any big decision, and maybe that's why he'd stick to it so firmly. That's not to say that every choice is always going to be a good one, but he knew how to take responsibility for the choices he made.

This isn't all your fault. I'm helping my parents with the forms to close out David's life insurance policy, since he was still under their policy. Everything happened a week ago, but it's ongoing until the full investigation of the cause and circumstances of death can be completed. There would have been an investigation anyways, since the owners of the bar have their own insurance. I know that insurance companies aren't in a hurry to pay things out, but a part of me hopes that all of the investigations and all of the reports will be helpful for my parents. Not everyone gets this level of detail when they lose someone. So you have everyone's insurance crawling over each other to get to the truth of what happened, and your obituary runs in this middle of me having to get all the forms to all the people in duplicate or triplicate or whatever. I'm trying to make sense of everything, and then I see the obituary. An obituary that could have been written about anyone.

I have the initial police report here, but I could almost quote it by memory at this point. According to the police report, the fire started at approximately 9 that night. The wiring behind the south wall of the building had been frayed for some time, based on the condition of it all. The report estimates that a combination of excessive heat with the abundance of dry wood near the wiring led to the initial spark. The language is very clinical and dry, but tinder box is the phrase that comes to mind for me.

Reading the report, I want there to be more. I want there to be a crooked contractor trying to make his way into a bigger profit or some plan by the owner to make extra money. It doesn't sound like any of that happened. The reality is that the bar was probably built to the bare minimum standards of the law and there probably hadn't been a thorough inspection in the last ten years. In a place like that, it didn't take long for the smoke to get thick and to get everywhere. It was made worse by the fact that the windows were shut at night. The police report quotes a witness saying they saw David outside at the dumpster, tossing a bag in as smoke started to pour out from the building. Most of the witnesses didn't know David or anything, but a few people remember someone pushing his way through the crowd while everyone tried to get out. A couple others saw a man matching David's description carrying a woman out of the building.

I was trying to fall asleep last night, but I kept thinking about how not everyone was able to corroborate why David ran back into the bar. The day after the fire, my parents get a call to the house from a woman who says she worked with David. She tells them that he ran back in because he thought someone needed help, and I believe that.

A lot of people die for no reason. Every day, you have acts of God or senseless tragedies that don't really explain what happened. For David though, it couldn't be more clear as far as I can tell. His death was the sum total of everything he tried to be, of all the choices he knew he needed to make. I can wish my brother was still here, but I can't be mad about that last choice he made. I can't imagine him doing anything else.

Even though I still picture that casket lowering into the ground, I catch myself forgetting sometimes that he's gone. Then it all comes rushing back. He isn't working or off doing something—he's just gone. No obituary was ever going to be good enough, but I just hope you can understand him a little better.

Message Received: June 15th, 2:31pm

ISAAC—I DON'T KNOW IF THIS IS REALLY YOUR JOB OR NOT, but I read the obituary written for the man who died in the fire last week. My name is Isaac and I used to work at a shoe store with David. I got to know him pretty well over the years. We both worked the morning shift, when there usually weren't many customers on the weekdays. This was a few years ago, but we'd kept in touch since then. Something about him being summed up so quickly in yesterday's paper made me want to give you a call.

When I heard what happened, it fit. Given everything I knew about the guy and all the conversations we had, it made sense.

David was a great guy, even if he did tend to take things pretty seriously. No one ever died from not having their right size shoe, but he was always focused any time a customer asked him for help. I had to talk to him about that a couple times, since digging through a truckload of boxes to find that one pair isn't always the best use of anyone's time. He didn't seem to mind though.

I took another job not too long after my wife became pregnant, but I really enjoyed working with him. Not everyone would let me just babble on about movie trivia for hours. I never did ask him if he also liked the random movie trivia that I talked about, or if he was just too nice to interrupt me. After I read about him in the paper, it occurred to me that I don't think I bothered to ask him very much at all.

Even when we no longer worked together, I was still his go-to for any reference he might need. It took almost a year of working practically the same hours before he started to warm up to me, so maybe I was one of only a few people to get that far.

When my wife Lisa and I got married, we had our honeymoon in Australia. I used to talk a lot when we worked together, and it wasn't long after Lisa got pregnant that I started telling people how I wished we had thought to get a stuffed koala or stuffed kangaroo or something; we were married about a year before she got pregnant, but I was telling people that I wished I'd thought ahead. David had been working the day of the baby shower, but we did get a box from him. I must have told everyone I knew about wishing I could find a stuffed koala or kangaroo, but he was the only person who'd thought to go online and look for one. I wish he could have seen Lisa's face when she opened the gift and saw that stuffed koala.

And I know what you might be thinking. "How hard is it to go online and find a stuffed koala?" You're right. Everyone who has said that over the years is right, it's not hard at all. Now ask me how many other stuffed koalas or kangaroos we got for that baby shower? Just the one from David. I'm sorry, I just get a little prickly when someone tries to downplay the little things like that. Just because he didn't move heaven and earth doesn't make it meaningless. Just because his obituary was forty-four words long doesn't make him meaningless.

Message Received: June 15th, 11:28 pm
TESS—ONE MORE THING: DAVID HAD A MEMORY like I couldn't believe. He'd remember the most random things, and then bring them out later on. Especially quotes and expressions. I don't know if he would even call it his favorite expression, but it sure seemed to pop up a lot. "The greatest gift God gave man was choice". I'm not even sure where he got that from – it sounds like the kind of thing my grandma would have had embroidered on a throw pillow.

Choices. He liked to talk about how we are the choices we make. Anyone can talk, and that's all some people do; for David, the real measure of someone was what they decided to do. I think that David liked the idea of being able to shape who he was. If we are the sum total of the choices we make, doesn't that mean we also have to accept those choices that don't pan out the way we might have expected? Seems like David's kind of idea for figuring out the world.

When I think about how much David focused on choice, I have to come back to that last choice he made. In the days since the fire, everyone wants to Monday Morning Quarterback everything. I have no intentions of going back to that job even if they do rebuild the place, but every single inspector or investigator needs to talk to me. That's what happens with this sort of thing, I guess.

I've had to tell the story so many times, what difference does once more make? So here goes. Last week on the 5th, someone's kid got sick so I ended up getting a call to come in and work a shift on my night off. As far as I know, David had always been planning to work that day.

David was the one who first smelled something. He said it smelled like burning plastic, but I didn't smell anything. I'd been taking a group of 21-year-olds through a "sampling" of cheap liquor, so maybe my nose was just dulled by that point. Or maybe he was just always a step ahead of everyone. The bar was pretty packed, at least for a weeknight, so I eventually told him he was crazy with the smell. None of the customers had smelled anything, but they weren't exactly sober either. It was probably around 8:30 when the food orders started coming in pretty fast, so I banished him back to the kitchen. When you have enough drinking, there's going to be a rush on food. I can only imagine that he was distracted with the burgers and the fries, focused on cooking with the same intensity he had for just about everything else. Sometimes I'd peak into the kitchen when he was really busy, to see him working the stove like he could be in two places at once if he just tried hard enough.

By the time I noticed the burning plastic smell, I suppose it was already too late. I don't remember if I actually shouted anything into the kitchen or if I just meant to, but David would have been taking the trash outside at that point anyway. It was about nine, but I wasn't exactly watching the clock. Most other Tuesdays, it might not have been that bad. Sure, people are going to freak the fuck out, but ten freaked out people can be managed a bit easier than forty.

I remember fire drills from elementary school. This idea that any group of people could calmly and orderly leave some place once a fire started—well there's a reason the saying "cry fire in a crowded theater" isn't synonymous with an organized departure. There was pushing and shoving, and one of those 21-year-olds knocked me over while she rushed for the door. In a situation like that, I don't think

I'll ever have the right words for it. I was on the floor, and I had already started breathing in the smoke. I tried to get up a few times, but people knocked into me and no one stopped to help.

Things were hazy and I was coughing bad. The place had gotten quiet except for the sound of the fire. I tried to get up on my own, but the smoke was already so thick that my eyes burned and it felt like coughing was all I could do. Then I felt someone's arms lift me up off of that disgusting bar floor. I remember seeing him as soon as we cleared the smoke. He was coughing worse than I was, since he kept me low while he carried me out. His face was covered in soot, but I remember hearing someone shout that they thought there was still somebody inside. What's worse than shouting fire in a crowded theater? Maybe making a person like David think that someone would die if he did nothing. Maybe that's worse.

Message Received: June 16th, 1:28 pm
GREG—HI, MY NAME IS GREG and I just wanted to call in about the man who died in the fire. I knew David all through Jr. High school and we were friends in that awkward kind of way you become friends with people in Middle School. It's a foregone conclusion if you have enough classes together and someone isn't too weird, so you just kinda go with it. I guess it wasn't until we got into High School and I saw how everyone else started to change that David really stood out. He was reliable in a way that most people aren't, especially not when hormones start hitting you like a sack of potatoes. We stopped having classes together as much, and it's too easy to find a reason not to make the effort. It's easy to not invite someone over anymore and just stop making room for them in your life, because you have new friends. Then you get to a point where you haven't seen someone for years, and you hear about him dying. Then you stay up half the night thinking about that friend of yours you used to walk home from the bus stop with until you started driving.

I didn't go to the funeral and I wouldn't have felt like I belonged there anyway, but I did pick up the newspaper on Friday to read the obituary. I don't even know why I felt the need, and it was probably more out of just wanting to know a little more about the man David grew into after High School. I think I wanted to see how the guy I'd known grew into the man who ran back into a fire.

My husband loves those crime shows on TV. He's always trying to get me involved in whichever one is the next big thing, but there is an appeal to it all: those shows always have easy answers and someone to blame. You're not going to draw someone in for sixty minutes if it all boils down to some act of God. On those crime shows, there's always an army of highly-trained professionals tracking down the answers. There are always answers to find, too. It would have been some nefarious scheme, where David gets caught in the middle.

Even before the obituary came out, I started reading all the articles that had been written about what happened. I wanted there to be some deeper meaning, for him to have had some deeper meaning. But then you happen upon five words that they never use in those crime shows: no foul play is suspected.

I don't know why I called or what I really wanted to say. It's hard to put your finger on what makes someone like David different. If you'd asked me a year ago, I don't think I would have had a good answer for you. After thinking about it though, it all makes sense. When you have a flood of people all climbing over one another to get out of a building, it makes sense for David to run back in.

Message Received: June 16th, 11:15 pm
Tess—OK, ONE MORE THING. I'VE BEEN THINKING about all of the ways that it could have changed. If he hadn't run in to get me or if I'd listened to him about the smell or if he hadn't thought someone else was in there or if any number of other things were different. But none of it matters as long as David is still there when the fire starts, and as long as David is still David. David is always going to be running back into that building to try and save someone. Don Quixote is always going to be tilting at windmills. Change any number of things, and he always runs in there to help—he always risks himself, because we are the choices we make.

Maybe none of this really matters and maybe you don't care, but I've been thinking about David's obituary ever since I picked up that paper. Eventually there's going to be a point where everyone who really got to know him is gone, and all that will be left is that obituary. And fuck me I guess, but those forty-four words just aren't good enough.

IN LOCO PARENTIS

BEFORE I TURNED EIGHTEEN, I KEPT WAITING for my birthday to come along so I could feel like something major had shifted inside of me. It's been a month now and three weeks since graduation, but the biggest change so far is that I can work the late shift to help fold clothes at the end of the night. After everyone has clocked out, we stand around the large glass doors in the near-darkness while Shelby puts in the security code for the alarm.

"Alright, everybody," she says, as we shuffle outside. Shelby pulls the big glass door hard behind us, waiting for that metallic click. A few people walk toward their cars, but Shelby stands around as though it was her plan all along. She doesn't ask if I want her to wait with me, because I get the feeling that she wouldn't let any of the women wait alone in the parking lot after hours; Shelby isn't the type to ask a question if she already knows what she's going to do. Then she sees Peter's work van pull into view, the words *HVAC Repair* visible in the over-lit parking lot. "This you, Claire?"

"Yeah," I say, as Peter slows to a stop in front of the door. He's still in his work shirt, the white calligraphy of his name standing out against the dark blue fabric. Even in the darkness of the van, his red hair still somehow looks bright. "Have a good night, Shelby." I open the door and climb inside.

"Hey," Peter says, as I click the seatbelt into place. I nod at him, as he starts off in a big loop around the parking lot before shooting back out onto the main road. I close my eyes and lean against the headrest, listening to the country music coming through Peter's speakers. "Long day?" he asks.

"Yeah."

"Is that why you've been ignoring people?"

I pull my phone out of my jacket pocket, looking for a missed call or a message that hadn't buzzed. "Did you guys try and get a hold of me?" There's nothing from him or John, just several calls I've been putting off returning. The first call came from my aunt on my mom's side Tuesday, but this was at the end of a long day and I figured I would just call her the next day. Each time my phone would buzz again, it would be another far flung relative from my mom's side calling. I wasn't trying to ignore anyone, but Peter's the only one who ever calls me without needing something. Even John, as sweet as he is, never calls; he'll send a hundred texts, but I don't know if he ever speaks on the phone with anyone except for Peter. Whatever my aunt or grandma or anyone else needed could wait.

"Not us," he says, "your aunt gave me a call."

"Jesus, you'd think somebody died." After I put the phone back in my pocket, I turn to Peter. "Has somebody died?"

"Kinda the opposite, actually." Peter chuckles to himself. "Story is, your mom's been born again. Again."

"Fourth time's the charm, I guess. So that's what's going on?"

"They want you to call her," he says simply, putting his blinker on to turn onto our street. All of the family who didn't think to send a card for my birthday are now rallying around this old cause? As though that's all there is to being family.

"If everything's so important, why isn't my mom the one calling me?"

"Would you answer?"

I shrug. "What'd my aunt tell you?"

"Not much," he says, pulling onto our street. "Just that your mom's doing better and wants to talk to you. Probably wants to reconnect, but that's just my gut."

Should I be annoyed that they'd reach out to Peter to get to me? Maybe I should have more questions, more anger, more of something at least. But I don't, and California feels so far away.

As Peter pulls into our driveway, I see the garage door is open and John is working on the old sedan. John got a good deal on it after a customer decided the repairs would be too much; he and Peter presented it to me as my big graduation present, promising that the bones were there for a reliable car. He's been spending the last month trying to bring the car back to life. With the starless sky above us, John's stand of work lights spill brightness out into the night. Getting out of the car, Peter walks into the garage as John pokes his head out from under the hood.

"Are you going to be out here for a while?" Peter asks, placing his arms around John's waist and kissing him on the top of the head.

"Probably a little while," John's focus is still on the engine, "but I'll shower before I come to bed."

"I appreciate that."

"How are things going, John?" I ask.

"Pretty confident I can get the car to not explode on you, Claire."

"That's awfully kind of you," I say, walking toward the door leading into the house.

"Letting cars explode is typically frowned upon." John smiles as I disappear into the house.

When I walk into the kitchen, I expect to see the sauce pan and dishes still in the sink from when I made my lunch before work; instead, all of the dishes from earlier are put away and someone gave the kitchen a nice cleaning. As I start to boil water in the saucepan, I open up the cupboard and grab the last package of ramen.

"We need some more ramen," I say, as Peter enters the house from the garage. "Do you have to work tomorrow?"

"No overtime this weekend." Peter sits down on the couch and picks up a book of crossword puzzles I got him for his birthday. "I need to work on the yard, but how about we go to the store in the morning?"

"Sure."

For as long as I have lived with Peter and John, we've always sat on the couch and watched TV while we ate. Even before I started working nights, the dinner table in the corner of the small kitchen was mostly for show. When I settle down on the couch, Peter nudges the remote toward me without bringing his focus up from the book. Once my ramen has cooled down enough, I eat quietly with the TV's volume low.

When my phone starts to buzz, Peter grabs the remote to mute the TV. I don't reach for the buzzing phone though, instead becoming very fascinated with my toes until the phone quiets. After a moment, Peter unmutes the TV and sets the remote back on the coffee table.

"Are you gonna ask me about things?" I ask.

"I wasn't planning on it." Peter turns the TV off, also setting the book of crossword puzzles down. "You want me to?"

"I don't know." When I came out to Indiana, everyone was so panicked. My phone was blowing up for days; things only calmed down when all of the extended family at least came to terms with the idea of Peter and John looking out for me. I heard from aunts and cousins and just about everyone, except my mom. "No one's left a message, but I know what they'll say if I call them back."

"Yeah."

"Should I call her?" He has to know what I'm really asking. The extended family eventually decided on the idea that I'd go back to California once my mom got her act together, but I only ever agreed to that by not objecting too loudly. It started as a temporary plan for six months, and then to finish out my junior year. And then my senior year was underway, and I didn't hear from anyone on that side of the family until two days ago. I wondered for a while if they had forgotten about me, but apparently not all the way. Do I give up everything I have here in order to meet some familial standard I never fully agreed to?

"Do you want to?"

"Not really."

"Then don't." Peter takes a drink of his water, resting it on his knee after he's done. "I've heard all of it before, from a shit ton of people. Everyone likes to talk about family and forgiveness, but they weren't there. They didn't see your mom leave you waiting at school, until I got home from work and realized no one had bothered to pick you up. They didn't see my dad kick me out of the house when he caught me kissing that boy from church. Some people can't see beyond their own ideas of family. Family is just people, and some people can be shitty. Do with that what you will, Kid."

"So no one can change?" It's not even that I think religion is going to make a difference. It never did before, but there is something tempting about the idea that the mother I remember has come to look more like the kind of mother my friends had. As though it just took losing me for a little while to shake things up, and now she's better.

"My dad sure as hell won't." Peter finishes the last of his water. "But maybe your mom did change, and that's up to you. Just don't do anything because you think some people get a pass. Being an adult means you can choose who's in your life." He places his glass on the coffee table. "I'm happy to tell them to fuck off if they keep hounding you."

"Thanks, but I'll manage."

"Alright," Peter says, picking his book of crossword puzzles back up. "Any news on the junior college?"

"I got everything submitted, so now I just have to wait for financial aid." It's not even the end of June, but he's been on me about junior college even though I haven't received my high school diploma in the mail yet. He didn't try to talk me into applying to universities at the start of my senior year, not after that fight we got into when I told him that those schools decide who does and doesn't belong before they even read the application. He never let up about college in general though. At my graduation dinner, he stuffed a pamphlet for the junior college into the gift bag that he and John had gotten me. It was just the three of us, and my phone didn't buzz that whole night.

"Let me know," he says, "We'll make it work."

"Thanks." I still sometimes think about saying that junior college just feels like high school with ash trays or I want to point out that he's happier working in HVAC than most people who get a Bachelor's, but we've had those conversations. He'll say I can do better, but I don't know. It's hard to keep arguing with the only person who thinks you'll amount to anything. At least he didn't argue with me when I said I wanted to stay local, instead of looking at options back in California. "Can I use your laptop to check my application?"

"Sure," Peter says, and I grab the closed laptop from the coffee table.

When I log into the financial aid website, the only update is a red exclamation point next to my application, showing that it hasn't been submitted like I thought. When I scan through the application, I notice that I skipped a question toward the end of the form: *Are you claimed as a dependent by a parent, guardian, or anyone acting in loco parentis?* No wonder I'd skipped over it when they started using Latin. When I groan, Peter looks up.

"Problem?"

"Probably not. I don't suppose you know any Latin?"

"Try me."

"In loco parentis?"

"In place of a parent." He doesn't hesitate, and he grins at what I imagine to be the look of shock on my face. "It has to do with legal guardianship."

"Does Latin come up a lot at work?"

"It's your fault," he taps the book resting on his knee, "they always include Latin phrases. For the record, ad hominem and habeas corpus pop up a lot."

"Thanks." I click *No* next to the question, and then hit the submit button.

MY FIRST MEMORY OF PETER IS FROM THIS NIGHT when my mom dragged me to a new church on a random Thursday, seemingly convinced that things could still turn around for us. This was after my dad had died, and my mom learned the hard way that too many men will pretend to not mind that you have a kid for only so long;

eventually the truth is going to come out, and they'll either leave or make you wish they had. In between a string of bad boyfriends, my mom took to the idea that religion was the thing we had been lacking in our lives. Before the dry sermons and the lifeless psalms, before the narrow minds and the judgement, they shuffled everyone younger than seventeen into different rooms for youth group. Peter and the minister's wife were the oldest ones in the room, and it wasn't until later that I ever wondered why he preferred helping supervise the younger kids when all the other teenagers were in the next room.

In between making crosses out of yarn and popsicle sticks or coloring pictures of the apostles, we played a game called "Guardian Angels." Standing in a circle, some of us would be blindfolded and told when to walk forward. The trick was that each blindfolded child had a guardian angel to guide them safely from one side of the circle to the other, usually leading their peer with guiding hands on the shoulder. Most of the guardian angels would walk slowly behind their charge, laughing with amusement anytime we would bump into one another. The blindfolded children and the guardian angels would change up every time, but sometimes Peter would join in with the younger kids.

I was ten at the time, shifting nervously while the minister's wife tied her scarf snugly over my eyes after one of the regular blindfolds had gone missing. Standing at the edge of the circle, I could hear laughing as feet shuffled across the industrial-grade carpet.

"I've got a plan," Peter said softly, "When I say go, run straight into the circle ok?"

"What?" I whispered, not sure if talking was allowed.

"It's ok." His hands gripped my shoulders softly, but firm. "I've got you."

I could feel Peter waiting, but he didn't say anything else. As the other children shuffled through the circle, I tensed up.

"Alright…Go." His hands gently shoved me forward. Under the hazy red of the scarf, I could only make out the vaguest of shapes.

I charged forward into the circle as fast as I could. The minister's wife gasped as I ran forward; I could hear the other children as I passed, so close that I felt the brush of someone's sleeve when I ran by. I would only put it all together later that the sound of feet in the distance was Peter running to the other side of the circle.

"Whoa." Someone said as I ran past, but Peter's arms were already opening up to catch me as I made it through the circle. I waited, until Peter began to undo the blindfold and handed it back to the minister's wife.

"Hey." I felt his hand on my shoulder again, as the minister's wife shook her head disapprovingly at him. "Were you worried?"

"Not really."

"Good." His hand squeezed my shoulder softly.

I didn't know that my mom was in the main chapel at the time, with all of the other single parents looking for a Godly partner. Peter's father was in that same chapel, trying to pretend as though his fresh divorce and recently dropped assault charges were all part of God's plan. After the minister's wife walked away, I looked up at Peter for the first time. His red hair and broad shoulders made him look like some ancient Celtic warrior, newly welcomed into the church. Even at sixteen, he towered over all of us and looked like he'd already begun to shave.

Our parents married just two months later, throwing Peter and I together without any thought. Before my mom saw through her new husband's thin veil of godliness and he saw through her flimsy attempts at wifely duties, I had a stepbrother six years my senior. First through their honeymoon period and then through their marital strife, they left Peter to look after me. When the marriage fell apart about four months after the cotton anniversary, Peter had already been kicked out of the house. When my mom and I drove away from Peter's dad's house and toward the next big idea that would solve all of our problems, I thought about that first moment of Peter's hands on my shoulders. That's how I knew I could count on him, even after more than 3 years passed without seeing him.

And then one day I was on a bus, with about a hundred dollars' worth of crumpled bills and Peter's address written on the inside of a notebook. It was only after the bus left California and drove into Nevada that I realized I couldn't remember when the idea had started. People want there to be a single moment, but the truth is that it builds up over time. There won't always be a big fight or a shitty boyfriend, and sometimes it's worse to find yourself writing checks in your mom's name so that all the bills get paid. Surviving off of the combination of my dad's life insurance money and alimony payments from Peter's father, barely getting by was always enough if it meant she could avoid putting in any extra effort. It gets exhausting to look at the woman passed out on the couch and realize that you don't even know when she stopped thinking of herself as a mother. It made sense to swipe a five or a ten from her purse, something small that she could blame on a generous tip or a greedy cab driver. As my bus passed into Utah, I shoved down that tiniest tinge of guilt at leaving my mom without anyone to look after her. I tried to convince myself that it wasn't fair for her to put that on me and sometimes I believed it.

When a sign announced that the bus had crossed into Nebraska, my thoughts turned to Peter. All of the faith that had evaded me in church started to manifest as the bus drove, and I knew he'd recognize me even though I felt impossibly removed from the stepsister he'd last seen. When I arrived at the address copied off of an old Christmas card and knocked on the door, he stepped to the side and made room for me in the two-bedroom house he and John had recently purchased. That was nearly two years ago, and I still wonder how long it took my mom to notice I had left.

BY THE TIME I WAKE UP, MY PHONE has collected a few more missed calls. At this point, the idea of answering any of these calls feels more counterproductive than anything else. We'd pretend to catch up for a little bit, before the conversation would veer toward my mom. And then I'd be reminded that the idea was only ever that I live with Peter temporarily, and certainly not for this long. Maybe she really has changed in these last couple of years and needs me or misses me or thinks that she can do better. Maybe I'd answer if any of these people calling bothered to remember me aside from these little family emergencies. Maybe I'd answer if any of the family calling me now could tell you anything about who I am.

When I walk into the living room, John and Peter already have cups of coffee in front of them on the coffee table as they sit on the couch. With my shifts at the store and the overtime Peter's been putting in lately, it's become rare that all three of us have any days off together. John's head leans against Peter's shoulder, his black hair looking even darker so close to Peter's red hair.

"Morning."

"Morning, Claire."

"Morning," Peter takes a drink of his coffee, "How do you feel about leaving for the store soon?"

"That sounds good." I walk past them into the kitchen, pouring some milk into my mug before filling it to the brim with coffee. I take a drink from my mug, walking back into the living room. "Are you going to come with us, John?" I sit down at the far end of the couch from Peter and John, placing my feet up on the coffee table.

"Nah," John takes a drink of his coffee, leaning his head back on Peter's shoulder afterward. "I think I'm close with your car. With a bit of luck, I might have that thing roadworthy in a few days."

I almost thank them again for the car, for what must be the hundredth time, but they would both play it off with the kind of Midwestern humility that I think attracted Peter to the state in the first place. I just smile at them both, and get up to change into real clothes. After I've changed, I come back out to find Peter alone on the couch and the sound of classic rock gently seeping in from the garage. Peter sets his book down on the coffee table, and we both head out to the work van.

While Peter's driving, I'm too busy thinking about things with my mom to notice at first that he goes by the Save-A-Lot we normally shop at.

"Are you ok if we just go to Kroger?" He asks, "I'd rather not stop too many places."

"Sure," I say, as he puts his blinker on to turn into the parking lot of the Kroger. I follow Peter through the large glass doors, but I start to wander to the left as soon as he grabs a basket.

"You need stuff?" He raises an eyebrow.

"Maybe. I thought I'd look around."

"Ok, just try not to take too long."

After I wander around for a minute, I find myself heading toward the deli counter. I hadn't planned on it, but I grab a tenderloin and it feels weighty in my hand. It's on sale, and it doesn't seem like such a bad idea to get a cart for myself. I go back to the vegetable section and grab onions, potatoes, carrots; all of the things that look just a little better than those same vegetables at Save-a-Lot. On my way to find Peter, I pass by the desserts and throw a cheesecake into the cart as well.

There are only a few things that Peter refuses to get at Save-A-Lot. Macaroni and Cheese is at the top of that list, and no one could convince him that the off-brand stuff tastes as good as that name brand blue box. So it isn't any surprise to find Peter in the pasta aisle, scooping an armful of blue boxes into his handheld basket alongside a tub of butter and a pack of ramen.

"What's all this?" he asks, seeing my cart.

"Just some stuff." We start walking toward the registers at the front of the store. "Maybe we have a real dinner for once?"

"You got enough for all of that?"

"It won't be that much." I'm already doing the math in my head though, trying to remember what my account balance is as I unload the cart. Did that phone bill already come out or is it on the 13ᵗʰ? Did I already give Peter my share of the electricity bill? I can feel Peter's eyes on me as he places his stuff on the conveyor belt and the cashier rings up everything from my cart.

Peter sees me take a deep breath when I see things total up to $35.76, reaching for my debit card. He removes the plastic divider between our items, stepping in front of me toward the cashier. "This is all together." The cashier looks at Peter as though she's about to say something, but she just shrugs and presses a button to keep adding things.

"Peter..."

"Don't worry about it, Kid." Peter hands the cashier his debit card, as I push the cart forward in time for the cashier to start loading the bags in. We don't say anything else until we're back home and Peter is pulling into the driveway. From the van, I can see John's feet sticking out from under the car.

"We're back," Peter shouts from the driveway as he exits the van, and John waves a foot in our direction.

"Do you have any other plans today?" I ask, grabbing two grocery bags as I exit the van.

"Nah." He grabs a few bags from the van and walks past John into the kitchen. "Just working on the yard a bit. You need something?"

"I just want to make sure you'll be around for dinner." I follow Peter into the kitchen, closing the door behind me. "How about the three of us eat at the table tonight?"

"So is that what the food's all about?" Peter asks.

"I got into a mood," I say, "It's just...do you remember when our parents went on their honeymoon and my grandma watched us? Those big dinners she made, especially Sunday?"

"Yeah."

"I thought it'd be nice to try something like that."

"Yeah, I get that." He starts unpacking the bags. "John and I will be here."

NOT LONG AFTER I'D COME TO INDIANA, I had a boyfriend for a while who wanted to do every little thing together. Even after the sex or the drinking or anything interesting, he still wanted to hang around. He'd offer to drive me to run boring errands like going to the store, following after me as I gathered the week's groceries into a cart. It ended about six months in, when I noticed that the fact that his family had their shit together weirded me out in a way I still can't quite articulate. I couldn't shake the feeling that I'd never be anything more than that girl from California he'd dated for a while; it's not even that I wanted a future with him, I just couldn't see someone like me ever fitting into a family like his. Not when the best furniture that we own came from the thrift stores closer to the rich neighborhoods.

I sometimes wonder how much of what I grew up seeing on TV is just commonplace for everyone else. Anytime a couple of characters are putting together an elaborate meal, I'll watch the mom share some time-honored family recipe and I always want to know if this is the way things are for everyone else. Am I the only who doesn't have recipes handed down from a long line of mothers and grandmothers? I search online for a pork tenderloin recipe that looks easy enough and I prop my phone up on the counter to shuffle through a 2000's playlist as I work through the steps. The sound of pop music from my childhood fills up the kitchen while Peter and John continue to focus on their own work.

John and Peter come back into the house a little after five, and I've already got everything laid out on the table by the time they've had a chance to wash up. They both open beers, and John slides a bottle of the fancy soda toward me. We don't get it that often, but occasionally John will sneak a six-pack into the cart while we're shopping and Peter will act like he didn't notice. Between the tenderloin and all the vegetables, the whole spread doesn't look bad for a first try. It reminds me of visiting friends' houses when I was younger, on those occasions where I remembered that not everyone ate TV dinners on a regular basis while their mom got ready to go out.

"Do you guys want to say grace or something?" John asks, looking from me to Peter.

I look at Peter for a moment, and I want to ask if he's also thinking of all the times his father made us close our eyes at the dinner table to say grace. Does he think of sitting in church on Sunday morning, wondering if those sermons of love and compassion would be enough to stop the shouting at home? Maybe Peter wonders if anyone asked about him after his dad kicked him out of the house. My mom and I stopped going to that church right as the marriage neared its end, and I wondered for a long time if any of my friends from youth group ever asked about me. I don't think they did.

My phone buzzes again, stopping the music that had almost

fully blended into background noise. When I get up from the table and walk to the counter, it's a number from the 209-area-code that I don't recognize. It's got to be my mom though, because a new voicemail pops up not long after the phone stops buzzing. I swipe at the screen to clear it, and turn off the music. "Nah. Let's not do grace," I say as I sit back down, and Peter rises slightly to cut a few chunks off the tenderloin. He places them on my plate first, before slicing off some pieces for him and John. We each scoop some of the vegetables onto our plates.

"Good job, Kid." Peter says, and John just smiles at me.

ACKNOWLEDGMENTS

I first want to thank everyone at Stephen F. Austin University Press for their help in making this collection come to life, especially Katt who worked with me as this collection continued to evolve. I also want to thank HoosierLit for publishing an earlier version of "Patchwork" in Vol.1, no.2.

I owe a considerable amount of thanks to the variety of mentors I have had in my life, both in the world of writing and beyond. As an early mentor in my graduate studies, I owe thanks to Dr. Victoria Lowell who always believed in and supported me through my educational journey. Thank you Dr. Donald Platt for allowing me to audit your poetry course, and for providing encouragement as I applied to MFA programs. I want to give special thanks to R. Dean Johnson as my advisor during my time at the Bluegrass Writers Studio and Julie Hensley for her support as a member of my thesis committee; their guidance was invaluable as I developed out many of the stories that comprise this collection. Everyone at the Bluegrass Writers Studio, both students and faculty, helped my writing develop significantly, and I am confident that this collection would not exist without all of the great feedback I received during my time at the program..

Thank you to my parents Jim and Teresa, and all of my family who continue to support me throughout my educational and writing career. Though I will always be thankful for my daughter, she deserves special thanks for always serving as my constant source of inspiration to be the best I can be in all aspects of who I am.

I want to thank those close friends of mine who have always been consistent and tireless supporters. I could easily list pages full of all the people who read and encouraged my writing over the years, but Kara especially deserves thanks for relentlessly supporting these stories as I tried to figure out what I wanted them to say and for supporting everything that this collection has become. I am quite confident that both these stories and I would be in much worse shape without you in my life.

Lastly, I want to thank those readers who decided to pick up this collection and read to the end. Thank you for investing your time in my stories.

CPSIA information can be obtained
at www.ICGtesting.com
Printed in the USA
JSHW021936091122
32912JS00004B/23